Toryn

By

Ronna M. Bacon

Psalm 32:7 You are my hiding place; You preserve me from trouble; You surround me with songs of deliverance.

NKJV

Table of Contents

Trudging through the bits of snow that still clung to the pavement, Toryn Knight headed for the back door of the police precinct. He was exhausted, he decided, as he keyed in his passcode. Stepping through into the building, the warmth hit him in a rush, a welcoming feeling after the coldness of the night. He stamped off the little bits of snow from his boots before heading for his office.

Toryn dug out his keys, unlocking his office door, and walking into the room. His briefcase was dumped on his desk before he reached to shed his jacket and toque, the garments hung on the wooden coat tree tucked into a corner behind his desk. His boots followed quickly to be set on the boot tray. Dress shoes were shoved onto his feet.

Sighing, Toryn stared around his office, exhausted beyond what he thought he could handle. It had been a long night and far from over. He squinted at the clock on his wall. Not even five in the morning. He sighed again, reaching for his mug and heading for the break room. He would find coffee there.

It was a somber building that he walked through. The overnight shooting with suspect robbers had left one officer dead and another officer critically wounded. The suspects had escaped in the confusion. That was not what any of them had wanted.

Toryn stopped by each officer and spoke with them, assessing them as to how they were. It was not a good place to be that morning. He turned back to his office, his coffee-filled mug set carefully down. He wouldn't be sleeping, he knew, his heart hurting for his officers. He ran his hands through his dark blond hair and then rubbed at his deep brown eyes. He had no idea what to say to them. Only God did. And he had to be that instrument between God and his men.

Looking around, Toryn felt a presence in the room with him even though he knew he was on his own. He looked up, a slight smile on his face. God was there and in the room with him. He looked around at a tap at his door and waved in the head of the detective team.

"Lyle?"

Lyle sat with his head bowed. He didn't have good news for the police chief.

"It's not good, Toryn. The other officer didn't make it." Lyle was sober as he watched Toryn's face as it grew even grimmer.

"Get me their contact information so that I can call on the families."

Toryn spent time in prayer before he was reaching for his winter outwear. He needed to walk through his town. He jerked his hat down his dark blond curls as trouble darkened his brown eyes. He headed towards the downtown area, hesitating as he approached a street corner. His eyes were watchful, looking for anything that seemed out of the ordinary. Toryn watched the young woman who stood on the opposite corner, her eyes focused down the street. She looked familiar to him but he wasn't sure that he even knew her.

Without warning the woman became to run towards Toryn, a terrified look on her face. Toryn raced in her direction, his eyes on her. He knew her, he decided before he reached her, his hand out to grasp hers. The beautiful Slaney Sullivan was in his town. He knew her from their university days. Her red gold hair and curiously shaded amber eyes had haunted him all these years.

"Slaney?" His hand reached for hers as he turned and ran in the opposite direction.

"Toryn? What?" Slaney could not utter anything more. Their steps pounded along the pavement as they ran from the men pursuing them.

Toryn looked for somewhere for them to hide, pulling Slaney towards a building where they would have found shelter, if they had made it in time. Shots rang out and the couple tumbled to the pavement with Slaney wrapped in Toryn's arms.

Screams and shouts rang through the early morning air as passersby ran to their assistance. A server from a nearby cafe rushed to the scene with clean towels to help control the blood flowing from the gunshot wounds. Horror showed briefly on the faces of the responding emergency services workers.

The physicians and healthcare workers scrambled as the stretchers were wheeled rapidly into the Emergency Department. It had been a brutal night and was not getting any better. Not one person had expected the chief of police to be one of the next ones injured.

Lyle headed for where Toryn was being worked on, worry on his face. He stopped just inside the door watching the frantic activity around his friend. He stepped back out of the room as an officer approached.

"Lyle? Do you know who the lady is?" Todd looked towards another room where hurried activity could be seen.

"Lady? No, I haven't gotten all the details yet." Lyle walked that way. "Do we have a name?"

"Slaney Sullivan."

"Slaney? Which one was the target? Toryn because he's the chief? Slaney because of her investigations?"

Both officers were familiar with Slaney's investigative reports. She didn't live in their town. Chances were that she was in the midst of an investigation that involved Oak City if she was in their town.

"Find out what you can. Aidan should be around here somewhere. And keep guards on them both."

Lyle walked away and towards the deputy chief who stood outside of Toryn's room, waiting for him.

Chapter 2

Lyle walked back towards where Toryn lay face down on a stretcher. He watched the hurried activity around his chief that had increased with the surgeon who was on call now bent over Toryn. His eyes moved to study Toryn's face and his own face grew sterner. He didn't like the gray look of Toryn's face or the blueness of his lips.

He then turned to the officer who stood nearby. This officer had been handed Toryn's police belt and then his shredded uniform shirt. The officer's fingers had tightened on the belt as he stared at Toryn's still form.

"Ted?"

Lyle's voice startled the officer and caused him to jump.

"Lyle?"

"Ted?"

"What happened, Lyle? We got the call but didn't know it was the chief." Ted looked around, not sure if he should stay or head for the department with Toryn's gear.

"I haven't heard all the details yet other than that Toryn was running away with the lady." Lyle frowned at that.

"Do we know who she is?" Ted looked up as the surgeon paused beside them.

"Toryn's people are here?" His voice was low but troubled.

"They should be." Lyle walked away to look for them, knowing that Toryn's parents were likely in the waiting room and anxious to see their son. He was correct. Tavin and Toria were on their feet, heading towards him.

"Lyle?" Tavin's voice was tight with worry.

"I'll take you to him. It's not a pretty scene." Lyle escorted them back before he walked out of the department and into the open air. He stood with a few white flakes of snow fluttering down. He didn't turn as he heard footsteps pausing beside him.

"How's Toryn?" Aaron Whyte, the deputy chief stood beside him, having been at the scene of the shooting until then.

"Not good. I had a chance to speak with the surgeon. One of the bullets is in his lung. The other? It's near the heart." Lyle continued to pray for his friend, knowing that God was in control.

Aaron grimaced. He knew only too well how dangerous that could be.

"Call Andrew McBeth. Phoebe needs to hear it from us. Even though it was proven she and Toryn are not cousins, they are still very close. I don't want her hearing from a news report."

"I will." Lyle walked away after a bit, watching the milling around of both on duty and off duty officers. Toryn was young to be a chief but he had risen rapidly through the force. He was a much-loved and much-admired chief, willing to go the extra mile for his officers.

Andrew McBeth, the police chief of the neighbouring town of Elmton, slowly pocketed his phone. He had not expected to receive a call from Toryn's father, Tavin. His wife, Phoebe, and Toryn had believed that they were cousins until it had been proven that Phoebe had been a stolen child. He rubbed at his face, a somber look on his face. Looking down, he smiled, the smile not quite reaching his eyes. His young daughter was holding onto a pant leg, the other arm raised to her daddy. Andrew swept her into his arms, feeling her tiny arms hugging him before she smothered him in kisses. He looked around as he felt a hand on his back and hugged Phoebe to him.

"Andrew?"

"Phoebe, that was Tavin." He could feel her shudder. "Toryn was shot this morning."

"Shot? Is he alive?"

"He is. But he is critical."

"Andrew! I need to get there!"

"And we will."

Tavin wrapped Toria in his arms as they waited for word on their son. Their minister, Gideon, had been around to pray with them. Andrew and Phoebe had arrived and sat nearby. Officers milled in and out, also anxious to hear about their chief.

Lyle stood a moment watching them before he walked down the hallway. He stopped at a doorway, his hand on the door. He prayed for the lady who lay in a bed in that room. He had met Slaney Sullivan before at a conference at a church even though she had tried hard to stay in the background.

Stopping by the bed, Lyle studied the lady. She was still sedated and that meant that he would not be able to question her that night. He was frustrated, to say the least. He wanted to solve the shootings and do that on that day. That was not going to happen.

Lyle looked up as Andrew approached him. Both men were praying for their friend.

"Lyle? I heard about your officers. What can we do to help?" Andrew rubbed at the back of his neck.

"To tell you the truth, Andrew, we have only just started the investigations. Then this with Toryn." Lyle leaned on the wall, suddenly overwhelmed and exhausted.

"It is a tough time. Our force will do everything that we can to help. I have Bill Buckley on it as well as Lily Gordon. They will head here sometime tomorrow to work with your people."

"And Caleb Logan is sending Frankie Brennan. We will solve the cases but it will take time."

Lyle walked away after time, leaving Andrew to find his wife again. Tavin and Toria were not there.

"Phoebe?"

"The nurse came for them. Toryn is in the ICU." Her voice quivered as she said that. Toryn had been a mainstay in her life and she was afraid to lose him.

All Andrew could do was hold her as she wept. He knew that the surrounding forces would stand tight with Oak City and would work with them to solve both crimes. A thought crossed his mind as to whether they were connected.

Chapter 3

Slaney Sullivan's eyes popped open and then just as quickly closed. The light in the room seemed too bright. She cautiously cracked one eye open enough to glance around. A hospital room? Slaney was confused as to why she would be there. She studied the intravenous line to her hand. Her head went back on the pillow. A hand found her shoulder before she frowned. What had she gone and done?

Footsteps startled Slaney before her head shot around and she stared in terror at the man who stood there. Aidan McNeill, police detective, watched her, not sure who she was or how it was that she had been chased towards Toryn. A dark look was on his face. He didn't want to be there. He wanted to be deep in the other investigation.

"Who are you?" Slaney's voice quivered with fear.

Aidan introduced himself, tucking the wallet with his police shield back into his pocket. Lyle had given him some information before sending him to interview Slaney.

"I don't understand why you are here." Slaney's face shuttered.

Aidan nodded. It was about what he had expected.

"I need to talk with you about the events yesterday morning. You were shot and we need to know if you know who it was."

"Shot?" Slaney stared at him in horror. "That can't be right."

"Trust me. It is only too true." Aidan waited for her to speak.

"I have no idea. I don't remember." Slaney stared back at Aidan.

Aidan walked away after not being able to get Slaney to speak with him. She had just stared at him without speaking. He paused for a moment, driven to pray for Toryn. Aidan headed towards the ICU, praying that Toryn had awakened.

Tavin turned as he heard footsteps, watching as Aidan approached him.

"Tavin?" Aidan was afraid to even a question.

"Aidan? You're still here?"

"I am." Aidan pointed to some nearby chairs. "Where is Toria?"

"She slipped home for a bit. She should be back soon." Tavin was grateful to get off of his feet. He had spent many hours pacing the hallways and standing at his son's bedside.

Aidan's eyes closed for a moment. Like his fellow officers, he was still in shock, mourning the loss of colleagues and also worried about their chief. Toryn was also a good friend of Aidan's.

"How is Toryn?" Aidan's eyes remained closed.

"He is still sedated. The doctor is still worried about him." Tavin watched as officers milled about, all looking for information on their chief. "What about the lady?"

"Slaney? She's awake but not saying much."

Toria approached the men, hearing Tavin's question. She turned and went on a hunt, looking for Slaney's room. She hesitated before the officer opened the door to allow her access into Slaney's room. Toria walked towards the bed, her eyes on the young woman. She had recognized the name. Toryn had talked about her during his university days, a special tone in his voice.

Her hand rested on Slaney's hair, praying for the young lady. Her eyes remained closed as she waited for God to speak.

Slaney jumped slightly as she felt a hand on her head. A mother's touch, she thought. She was unable to stop the trickle of tears that began. Slaney hadn't wept when she lost her parents and brother to a murder years earlier, a murder that was still unsolved.

Toria reached to hug the younger lady, a mother's kiss dropped on her hair. Toria prayed for her, her words whispering in Slaney's ears.

Slaney shoved away from Toria at last. She could feel a semblance of peace for the first time in months. She stared at the lady standing beside her bed. She was a stranger.

"I'm sorry. Do I know you?"

"No, I don't know that you do. I'm Toria Knight, Toryn's mother. I think that you were friends at university." She watched Slaney's face.

Slaney stared at her for a moment, memories fluttering through her mind.

"Toryn? We're friends. Where is he?"

Toria drew in a quivering breath. She was not even sure as yet that Toryn would even live.

"You don't remember? Toryn was shot yesterday protecting you. He's in the ICU."

"He was? He is? I don't remember." Slaney glared at the wall, distraught that she could not remember anything.

"It's okay, Slaney. It's who he is. He is our police chief."

"He is?" Slaney slumped back on the pillow a woebegone look on her face. "Can I see him?" She yawned and then slept.

Toria gave a small smile, her hand resting on Slaney's hair. She prayed for the younger lady before she walked away, heading for her son. Tavin wrapped her into a hug, feeling the sobs shaking her body.

"Toria, what happened?"

"Slaney. She has no one. It's so sad." She swiped at her face.

"She doesn't? We'll have to take care of her."

"We will. She was muttering as she went to sleep that her parents were dead."

Four days later, Tavin stood at his son's bedside, a hand resting on Toryn's hair. His prayers were raised for his son. Toryn was their only child. Tavin and his son were close. Toria and he were proud of their son but still worried deeply about his chosen career.

The ventilator had been pulled that morning and the medical staff was working on weaning him off some medications. Toryn was beginning to move restlessly. That was normal, he was told. His head turned slightly as he heard footsteps. Aidan stood beside him.

Aidan was exhausted. All of them had been working almost non-stop to find the robbery suspects and also the one or ones who had shot Toryn without success. It was draining on them. They were no closer to finding either party.

"Aidan? How are you?" Tavin was worried about his young friend.

Aidan shrugged. He was not sure any more how he was.

"How is Toryn?" Aidan studied his friend.

"They are weaning him off the medications. He is alive, praise God." Tavin wiped at his face. It had been too close to losing him.

"That is good. We are all praying for him. He's the best chief that we have had."

Aidan left shortly after that. He was exhausted and needed to sleep. He looked around as a hand landed on his shoulder. Don Devlin, a friend of his and Toryn's, stood there. He ran a security team whose members had gone through life and death adventures. He directed Aidan to a seat, shoving him down. Don then sat beside him, a prayer rising for his friend.

"Aidan? You need to head home."

Aidan gave a nod, his exhaustion evident. He had trouble focusing.

"Don? You're here?" Aidan blinked slowly.

"I am. I was worried about you. Come on. I'll give you a ride home. Lyle reached out to me." Don hauled Aidan to his feet and with a hand on his shoulder directed him outside to his truck.

Slaney watched the two men, standing nearby. She was going home that day and just didn't know how she would cope. She wanted to see Toryn before she left. She wasn't sure if this Toryn was the Toryn that she had been friends of sorts with at university. Slaney inched her way towards Toryn's room, a hand resting on the immobilizer that held her left arm still. Slaney then walked forward on silent feet to stand near Toryn. A sob rose within her as she finally realized that Toryn had indeed put himself in harm's way to save her. Her hand reached out to touch his face, surprised to find his face turning into it. Her hand then rested near the one on his chest, near enough to touch it. Slaney jumped as his moved to grasp hers.

Tavin and Toria watched from the doorway, shocked to see Toryn's unconscious response to

Slaney. This was not their son. He didn't date and was very careful in how he treated the ladies that he met. They moved closer just to see Toryn's eyes open and then focus on Slaney.

Tory blinked to focus, his eyes on the beautiful lady standing beside him. He knew her. It took a few moments before he spoke.

"Slaney? Are you okay?"

"I am. Thank you." Slaney watched as he struggled to stay alert.

Losing the battle, Toryn's hand tightened on Slaney's. He did not want to lose her.

"Don't leave me. Stay with me, Slaney." His eyes opened and closed. "I love you." He pulled down the oxygen mask and raised his hand holding hers so that he could kiss hers. His hand dropped back to his chest as he slept.

Slaney was in shock. Had he just done that? She caught a glimpse of a nurse replacing the oxygen mask on Toryn. She had just not expected him to do what he did.

Toria wrapped an arm around Slaney and pulled the younger lady from the room. She shook her head at Tavin as he followed them. They would talk later, she knew. Her priority at the moment was Slaney.

Tucked into bed in Toria and Tavin's home, Slaney slept. Her dreams were troubled at first until Toryn invaded them. Toria pulled the covers up tighter over the younger lady before she headed to find Tavin.

Tavin watched his wife, knowing that she would not leave Slaney. He himself was heading back to their son's side.

Lyle looked up from his desk. Aidan stood in his doorway before he entered.

"Aidan, you're supposed to be at home."

"I know. I just want to solve this." Aidan rubbed at his face. He knew that God was in control. He just wanted vengeance.

Lyle nodded. He himself had gone home only to come back. All the officers were like that. It didn't help that the police funerals were happening over the next couple of days. He prayed for his fellow officers. They needed their chief right now. Only Toryn could not be there for them.

"We all do. I talked to Tavin earlier. Toryn reacted to Slaney before they took her to their home. He woke up and spoke to her." Lyle didn't share what all Tavin had told him.

"He did? Do they know each other?" Aidan's head dropped back for a moment.

"Apparently they do from university. Toryn has never said but I always wondered if he had an interest in a lady somewhere." Lyle rubbed at his eyes. "He's going to be off for weeks."

"He will be but it will not stop him." Aidan cracked an eye open. "Do we know what Slaney does?"

"I heard that she works in the media but that is just a rumour. I have not been able to confirm that. Her life is very secretive."

Aidan nodded. Slaney kept her life very private.

"Tavin said that she would be with them for a few days. I'll drop by and see what I can find out."

Chapter 5

Three days later, Toryn was sitting up in bed. He had been moved to a bed on the surgical floor the day before. The staff was amazed at his recovery, but he brushed aside their comments. Toryn's eyes watched the door as he looked for a lady to appear. She just had not done so.

Tavin watched with compassion. He had asked Slaney to come with him but she had looked at him and then walked away. Slaney knew that she should go to see Toryn but she was not sure how to face Toryn after what he had said.

"Son?" Tavin waited patiently for Toryn to look at him. "When can you leave?"

Toryn sighed. He did not want to go home. He wanted to find Slaney but even more he wanted to find his officers. He had been dismayed that he had missed the funerals. Toryn had stared down George, one of the detectives, until George had gone to Aaron who had reluctantly provided the contact information for the families. Toryn had reached out to each one, despite the families' protests that he needed to heal. Aaron had also not been able to provide any further information on the investigations.

"Yeah, Dad?" Toryn finally looked at his father.

"When do you go home?"

"Tomorrow. Mom wants me to go to your place."

"That is likely a good idea." Tavin had a spark of mischief on his face. "By the way, Slaney is at our home."

Toryn's hand stopped rubbing at his face. *Thank you, Lord. She is not lost to me again.* He nodded, knowing that he'd need to speak with her. He had lost contact with her years ago. Sure, he could have used his resources to find her but knew that was unethical.

The next day, Slaney looked up from her laptop. She could hear other voices but shrugged. Her attention went back to the passage of Scripture that she had been studying. She needed to refresh her heart with God's promises.

Toryn stood and watched her, a hand gripping the doorframe. Don stood behind him, a tray of coffee and sweets in his hands. He waited patiently for Toryn to move into the room, a slight smile on his face. Toryn moved forward at last, his socked feet whispering softly on the wooden floor.

Slaney jumped at the slight noise, her hand closing her laptop. Her eyes were huge as she stared at Toryn, not taking it in that he was indeed standing in front of her. She watched as he dropped down on the couch. Slaney turned as she saw Don entering as well. On her feet, she moved rapidly away from the room before she came back to sit beside Toryn.

"Toryn?" Slaney's soft voice roused Toryn before he blinked at her. "Should you be here?"

Toryn nodded as his hand reached for hers.

"I need to be, Slaney. I have missed you."

—

"Toryn?" When Toryn didn't respond, Slaney was on her feet and walking away.

Don's eye followed her before he looked back at Toryn. He sighed to himself. *Here we go again*, he thought.

Toryn stared at Don before he took the mug of coffee being handed to him. He sighed as well. He wanted to go after Slaney but just didn't have the strength to do so. He looked up half an hour later to find Don had left.

Aaron and Lyle found seats in the office, sent that way by Toria. She quietly closed the door behind them before she prayed for the three. They were under tremendous pressure to solve the investigations. And they weren't really that much further ahead.

Lyle just bowed his head and began to pray, knowing that they needed God's guidance in this. Aaron picked up the prayer followed by Toryn.

Toryn raised his eyes, his worry hushed, feeling God's peace in the room. He opened his mouth and then snapped it closed. His hand took the folder that Aaron was handing to him.

"Before I read this, where do we stand?"

"Not where we would like to be." Lyle stared at Toryn. "We have little information on the robbery suspects. We're working it but information is sketchy. The car was stolen and wiped clean. We're interviewing witnesses over again but they aren't providing much more information than before."

"That was about what we had expected." Toryn glanced through the folder, pausing at the last page. "This name? Have you pulled her in yet?"

Aaron nodded, knowing that she was being interviewed.

"Aidan is questioning her now. We are hoping that she has some sort of information that will help."

Toryn nodded, knowing there were hours and days of intense work ahead of them to solve that incident.

"And your shooting, Toryn? We think it is related to Slaney. We have not found a lot of information on her. We can't find out what she does for a living." Lyle was puzzled by that. He had interviewed Slaney but had come away from that interview feeling as if the roles had been reversed.

Toryn gave a brief grin, remembering how quiet that Slaney could be about her life. It did not surprise him that Lyle had not gotten a lot of information from her.

"Slaney is like that. It has been number of years since I last saw her. I was surprised to see her that morning. I saw the men approaching her and ran her way. I didn't really know that it was her until I got close. I tried to save her." Toryn's face was sober.

"And you did just that, almost losing your own life." Aaron leaned forward. "What is the word on you?"

Toryn shrugged. The physician had been candid when Toryn asked about the long term of his health. The bullet that had lodged near his heart had caused damage to that area. The physician had been unable to give a prognosis on Toryn's health as it was too soon.

"We don't know as yet. It will be a number of weeks before we know for sure when I can return to work." His unspoken words hung in the air. There was a real possibility that he might never be able to take up the chain of command. That thought was sobering. He would need to pray it through and surrender his dreams and wishes to his Heavenly Father.

Lyle and Aaron walked away shortly after that conversation. They were at a loss. None of them could know just how diabolical the upcoming events would prove to be.

Toryn rose and stretched before he headed out to search the house. Slaney turned as he approached her only to find herself wrapped into his arms. Her arm around him helped keep them steady on their feet.

"Toryn?" Her soft voice caught at his attention and he hugged her tighter.

"How did we lose contact?" Toryn's question didn't need an answer.

Chapter 6

Slaney walked back into her apartment the next day, finding the apartment stuffy. She moved to open the windows. Slaney stood in her office staring at her desk before her laptop landed on it. She no longer wore the sling but still needed to be cautious in how she used the arm. Don had driven her home and walked through the apartment for her. He had hesitated before he left, wanting to say something but finding that Slaney didn't seem receptive to what he would say.

Apprehension was strong within her. Slaney had always been cautious in her work. Not even the publisher knew her full name, just her pen name. All her contact with him was through her lawyer. She suspected that the detective who had tried to interview her suspected that she wrote about true crime but he would not find her columns unless he did a lot of digging. Somehow she thought that he would just do that. Slaney had reached out to her lawyer, refusing to continue the interview without representation. Slaney had taken many steps to hide her identity from the public. She only could be contacted through her lawyer.

Two days later, Slaney headed out early in the morning. She had a favourite diner in the downtown area that would let her stay there for hours. Her favourite booth was at the back near the kitchen. The servers just kept her coffee cup filled.

Slaney set up her laptop and then was immersed in her writing. She didn't look around as customers came and went. Mary, the server that day, watched her and then simply kept refilling her mug of coffee and setting food down for her. She received a soft thank you each time.

Aidan and Don had been in the area, both searching for any information that they could find. It had not been planned for them to meet but they had agreed to have a coffee together and then spend some in prayer. They stared at Slaney for a moment before Mary approached them.

"Mary? Slaney's here?" Don just had to ask.

"Slaney? She comes in here a lot and just sits and does research or writes. I don't ask what she's working on. It's none of my business." Mary frowned at them.

"That's okay, Mary. We'll just join her." Don grinned at her and proceeded to do that. Aidan slid onto the seat beside him. They shared a look with one another when Slaney didn't even look up. That concerned them.

Slaney sensed someone sitting across from her but she was deep in what she was writing and refused to look up. She gave a thank you to Mary as a plate of food was set beside her. She ate as she continued to write, hearing men talking near her. Slaney shook her head. She was by herself, she decided, and those voices had to be coming from another booth.

Finally looking up, Slaney stared at Don and Aidan who were watching her intently. Her laptop was closed and then tucked into her backpack.

"What do you want?" Slaney didn't back down from the men. It was not in her to do that.

"Slaney? Did you even realize that we sat down here?" Aidan was shocked as she shook her head. "Slaney! Your life is at stake. You need to be aware of what is going on around you and who is there!"

Slaney stared at him, seeing Don's nod from the corner of her eye. She rose, her backpack on her shoulder.

"It's not your concern. I have lived for many years without your assistance. I will continue to do so." She walked away, stopping to pay for her food and then walking out of the diner.

Aidan stared after her before he turned to Don. He shifted to the seat where Slaney had been sitting

"She's got you there, Aidan. She won't speak with you and her lawyer. That much I'm reading from her."

"That's what she's said. And I have to speak with her again." Aidan was frustrated to say the least. "And Toryn is worried about her. How does he heal if he goes out there and tries to protect her?"

"How close are they?" Don had his ideas on that as did his team and their spouses.

Aidan shrugged at the question. He wasn't sure. He had heard from Tavin what Toryn had said.

—

That shocked Aidan. Toryn was not the type of gentleman who said that to any lady.

"I have no idea, Don. And I wish that I did. It would help." Aidan sipped at his coffee, setting the mug back down and wrapping his hands around it. "How close were they?"

It was Don's turn to shrug. He was good friends with Toryn and they had talked many times about their university days. He did not recall hearing Toryn ever mention Slaney.

"I have no idea, Aidan. We've talked about our friends from university. I don't remember hearing him say her name." Don stared out of the window, watching the vehicular traffic on the street. "It would make it easier to investigate if we did know."

"It would. I just can't get a handle on Slaney. And that's unusual." Aidan was on his feet, glancing at his watch. He was due back at the office for an interview with a suspect from another case. He just didn't want to walk away from what he was trying to find out about Slaney.

Don nodded as Aidan walked away, thanking Mary for a refill on his coffee. He looked up as Paul and Thomas, two of his team members, slid into the booth across from him. They didn't look very happy, he decided.

"Guys?" Don finally had to speak.

"We've been walking the downtown area. There's a contract out on Slaney. And she just doesn't seem to care." Paul was frustrated at that.

"Any reason for the contract?" Don was on his feet, heading for his truck, Paul and Thomas beside him.

"That we can't find out. We have no idea what she does for a living. And that is unusual. Word is that Toryn was shot because he got in the way. And now someone will be after him to take him out of the way." Thomas was thinking through what he knew. All he knew was that he didn't know a lot.

"I see. It's what we thought. We'll need to speak with both Slaney and Toryn." Don drove away, leaving the two men staring after him and then at one another.

"Toryn will be easy to talk with. Slaney not so much." Paul stated the obvious.

—

Chapter 7

Toryn roused the next morning, not moving for a moment as pain hit in waves. He sighed. He needed to be on his feet and active and that wasn't happening. Toryn had been warned severely that he needed to take this carefully. It was just not his character to do so, especially when it involved the men and women who served under him. He needed to be there for them and just wasn't able to. Toryn made a decision that morning before he rose that he would find his way to work that day, regardless of how much it hurt.

On his feet and showered, shaved, and dressed, Toryn carefully made his way to the kitchen. His father was waiting for him. He read his son correctly in that he wanted to see his people.

"Toryn? Sit and eat. Then, we'll pray." Tavin pointed to a chair. "Then, I'll take you to your office. You need to be there and your people need to see you."

Toryn sat carefully, knowing that his father was reading him.

"Thanks, Dad. I do need to do that." Toryn reached carefully for his fork and began to eat.

An hour later, Tavin pulled to a stop in front of the police department. He eyed the building and then his son. He reached out a hand to rest on Toryn's arm, bringing his son's eyes to his father.

"Let me pray for you, son. You're not well enough to be here. This is going to be extremely stressful. I understand why you want and, yes, need to be here. God will give you the strength and the words that you need. I will walk beside you as far as you will allow me to. It is not in your character to walk away from your people.”

Toryn kept his eyes on his father, knowing that his father was reading him correctly.

“It hurts, Dad. I should be here leading in this and I can’t. Not from my office.” Toryn blinked as he tried to control his emotions. “I know that I almost died. The surgeon was very open with me. And I know the limitations. But to not be involved is harder than being involved. And I do worry that we have not found the men responsible yet. Nor found the men who shot me. I worry about Slaney.” The tone of his voice changed as he spoke that lady’s name without his realizing it.

“You are worried and Slaney is worried about you. We need to get you two together again.”

“I know we do, Dad. She’s always been quiet about her life. I don’t know much about her. But I don’t want to see her hurt.”

“Toryn?” Tavin waited for his son to look at him. “Your mother and I were present in the room when you roused and spoke with her. We heard what you said to her. Do you remember what you said?”

Toryn thought for a moment and then shook his head. He could remember seeing Slaney and speaking but he could not remember what had been said.

"You told her that you loved her and then you kissed her hand." Tavin nodded as Toryn shook his head.

"I didn't say that. I wouldn't do that." Toryn was not a man who did that and to hear that he had? That shocked him.

"You did, son. Slaney has not said anything about it. And the way that I am reading her? She won't. She also won't hold you to it, thinking that you were disoriented and confused."

"I wouldn't do that, Dad. That's not me." Toryn was adamant that he had not done so.

"You did, son. You did. Slaney will take it and keep it in her mind but she will not expect anything from you. You said that you were only acquaintances."

"We were. She was not easy to get to know. She was part of our friends' group but kept to herself as much as she could. We never understood it." Toryn reached for the door handle and shoved the door open.

Tavin was around the car and helping his son to walk towards the building. Toryn hesitated before he walked into the building and found himself surrounded by his officers. Tavin stood back near a window and watched his son. That he was well loved and admired by his force as obvious.

Aidan watched for a moment before he approached Tavin. He knew the man well, Toryn being a good friend of his.

"Tavin? He had to come, didn't he?" Aidan shook his head at that thought.

"He did, Aidan. We couldn't keep him away. That would have been harder on him than coming here." Tavin rubbed at his cheek. "He's going to want to be part of the hunt even though he's not well enough to do that."

"We'll work with him on that. It's not easy to see someone you love hurt like this and almost lose them." Aidan walked away, sober thoughts chasing through his mind. He had seen that too many times over the years.

Two hours later, Toryn slowly walked back towards his father, fatigue evident in how he was moving. Tavin linked an arm with his son, leading him to the car and then helping him to sit inside it. Toryn's head went back on the seat as his eyes closed. He had overdone it, he knew, but he had had to come. His people had needed him.

Tavin pulled away from the curb, seeing the officers who had followed them from the building. They were worried about their chief, that much was obvious.

"We're heading home, Toryn. Not to find Slaney. You can't do anything more today."

Toryn sighed, knowing that his father was correct. He was exhausted. Yet the only person he wanted to find was Slaney. And he had no idea where she would be. Toryn needed to reach out to Don, who had told him that he knew where Slaney lived. He prayed that she was safe.

—

Slaney stood across from Tavin's home, watching as he helped his son out of the car and back towards the house. She frowned. She had not planned on coming there but her instincts had sent her there. Slaney rapidly walked towards the two men, Tavin pulling Toryn around.

Toryn simply reached for Slaney, wrapping her in a hug. He felt her hugging him back in almost a desperate motion. Tavin watched the two before he looked around and then with a hand on Toryn's back, shoved them towards the house. Someone was watching his son and he wanted him out of the open and under cover.

Chapter 8

Slaney paced Tavin's office, her arms wrapped around herself. She had no idea why she had felt the compulsion to be there. She really didn't. It must have been God, she decided. Turning around as she heard soft footsteps, Slaney faced Toryn. Toryn simply stood and stared at her for a moment.

Watching the conflicting emotions that momentarily flickered across her face, Toryn sighed. He need to talk with her but he had no idea what to say or how to approach her. He felt a hand on his arm, steadying him until he was forced to sit. Aidan had appeared at Tavin's request.

Aidan studied the couple before he shook his head. There was something going on between the two of them and he had no idea what. He had been unable to find out much about Slaney and that was very unusual. One of the detectives was still working on it. Other than the basics of her life before and during her university days, it was as if she didn't exist. That was puzzling them.

"Slaney? You and I need to talk." Aidan was adamant about that. "And now."

Slaney stared back at him, not backing down from him. She would not tell him about her life. She had taken too much time and trouble to hide who she was. Slaney had had to do that in order to protect herself.

"Really?"   Slaney walked past him and continued to walk out of the house. She stood by her car for a moment, watching the area around her. She could feel someone around her and felt fear for a moment. Jumping into her car, Slaney drove away, not seeing that Aidan had followed her.

Aidan sighed. This is not how it was to go. He turned back to find Toryn standing beside him, a dark look on his face.

"Aidan? Did you really have to do that?" Toryn was frustrated that Slaney had left.

"I need to interview her again, Toryn. We can't find any information on her after she left university. You know the drill, Toryn. We have to prove that she didn't have anything to do with either the robbery or your shooting."

Toryn nodded, fatigue weighing down his body. He knew that he had to sit down or lie down before he fell over. Aidan was correct. He did need to speak with Slaney and find out the information that was missing. He turned back to the house, Aidan's hand out to grip his upper arm and guide him inside to the couch.

Toria was waiting for them, a blanket covering her son as he stretched out on it, his eyes closing against the pain that he was feeling and the fatigue that was hitting him harder and harder.

Toria pointed to the kitchen and walked that way. Aidan hesitated and then followed her.

"Aidan? What happened? Where is Slaney?" Toria watched her young friend as he hesitated.

"She went home, I think. I just told her that I needed to speak with her and she walked away." Aidan paced the kitchen, distraught at what had happened.

Slaney dropped her backpack on her kitchen counter and then reached for a bottle of orange juice. Removing the cap, she took a long drink, recapped the bottle, and set it down on the counter. She paced through her apartment, feeling unsafe and also feeling as if someone had been in there.

Turning as she heard the doorbell, Slaney hesitated a moment before she walked quietly down the hallway to the door. Her hand rested on the door as she looked through the peephole. She frowned before she opened the door

"Don?" She was surprised to see him. She looked at the lady standing beside him, a lady around her own age.

"Slaney?" Don grinned at her. "May we come in? This is my sister, Daci. My wife, Delanie, is on her way. We just wanted to bring you a meal and pray with you. You've been a burden on our hearts since you were hurt."

Slaney stepped backwards to let them enter, surprised that they both hugged her as did the younger lady who had run up the stairs to join them.

—

"Thank you, I think." Slaney blinked for a moment. "I didn't expect this." She looked around, rubbing at her arms.

Don's face grew stern for a moment as he looked at Slaney and then shared a look with his wife and sister.

"Slaney? What are you feeling or sensing in here?" His hand on her arm stopped her from moving.

"I don't know, Don. I just feel as if someone has been in my apartment." She looked up at him, worry on her face for a moment.

"Let me look around. Is that okay with you?" Don waited for her to nod before he was searching the apartment. He didn't like what he was finding.

Delanie and Daci drew Slaney into the kitchen, placing the bags on her countertop.

"Slaney? Are you sure that you're okay?" Delanie hesitated before she asked that. "Don and I went through something before we married. I don't like to think that you're going through anything."

"It's happening whether you think I should be going through something or not." Slaney blinked for a moment, her eyes on Daci and then Delanie. "I have tried to keep my life private and it just doesn't seem that will be the norm for now. I don't like feeling as if I am in the spotlight."

"We know that, Slaney. We do know that. How be we eat and then spend some time in prayer? If you don't feel as if you can stay here, you can come and stay with me." Daci grinned at her. "Others of the ladies have done so."

"Thank you, Daci. This apartment was furnished when I rented it. I don't have a lot of personal stuff, by my choice." Slaney watched as Don walked towards her. "Don?"

"Someone has been in here, Slaney. I recommend that we pack you up and move you. Daci is correct. She has a very secure home and you would be safe there. She works for the women's shelter and can help you decide what you want to do and where you want to go."

Slaney took one look at him and then was almost running to pack. The three with her helped, moving the bags and boxes to Don's truck. Daci slipped into the passenger seat of Slaney's car as Slaney drove away and followed Don's truck. They didn't see the men who were approaching the apartment and then stopped as they entered her apartment to find her gone. That was not what they had expected to find. They had been assured that she was there and on her own.

—

Chapter 9

Toryn roused late that afternoon. He lay with his eyes closed, not hearing any movement around him. He sat up carefully, his hand resting on his chest. It was sore and Toryn was well aware that he had overdone it that morning, but he had needed to see his people and they had needed that as well. Aaron was taking care of what needed to be done but he simply stated that he missed Toryn in the office.

On his feet, Toryn headed for the office to drop down in the chair behind the desk. He reached for the mouse and woke up his father's computer. He hesitated for a moment before he began his own search for Slaney. He sat back. Aidan was correct. There just wasn't much information on her other than old addresses. What was she hiding? And how deeply was she involved in what had happened? Toryn didn't think that she had been part of his shooting. He remembered the look of fear on her face as she ran towards him. That was something that he would never forget.

Tavin watched his son, seeing the distress on his face. All he could do was pray for his son. He acknowledged that God was indeed in control of what had happened and where it would lead. Tavin turned as he heard Andrew's voice behind him.

"Tavin?" Andrew stopped beside him.

"Andrew? Is Phoebe here as well?"

"She is." Andrew nodded towards Toryn. "He's not doing well."

"No, he's not. He insisted on heading to see his people today. Slaney was here but left when Aidan told her that he needed to speak with her. She's hiding something and I don't want whatever it is to cause more harm to Toryn."

"None of us do. Maybe if Phoebe speaks with her?"

"She can try. I heard from Don. They moved her out of her apartment. Someone had been in there, he could tell. Nothing was placed as he put it."

Andrew nodded, knowing full well that would have happened.

"Don's put her somewhere."

"With his sister. Daci has really good security at her place, given her work."

"I know that she does. I've seen it. We'll head that way before we head home." Andrew walked into the office and simply sat in front of the desk, watching his friend.

Toryn looked up, his eyes blurring for a moment. He blinked, his vision clearing.

"Andrew? Is Phoebe with you?"

"She is. And you need to be in bed, not researching whatever it is that you were researching."

"I know, Andrew. I just want this solved. We're no closer to finding the robbers. The team is

—

working on it. And I know that they have been told not to talk to me."

Andrew began to laugh, drawing a smile to Toryn's face.

"We do that, Toryn. Phoebe's worried about you." Andrew wanted to relieve that worry for his wife.

"I know that she is. Even though it was proven that we're not cousins, I consider her family. I always will. Did you bring your little one?" Toryn had not heard a little child in the house.

"Not today. We will once you're getting better." Andrew looked down, praying for his friend. "What don't you know about Slaney?"

Toryn sighed, knowing that Andrew had gone to the heart of the matter and what he was trying to discover.

"There is nothing on her life after she graduated. No work listed. She seemed to completely drop off the face of the earth until she appeared here. I don't understand that."

"She's running, Toryn, and running from someone." Andrew studied his friend, seeing the understanding that crossed his face.

"She is and I want to help her. We were friends of sorts at university." Toryn paused for a moment to think back to those days. "She never really associated much with anyone, just kept to herself. I don't know why." Toryn rubbed at his face, not sure what to say.

"Talk to Emma. She may be able to help."

"That was my next thought. I just don't want to go behind her back to do so. If Aidan has, that was his call." Toryn knew that Aidan would make the decision that was needed. "Don sent a text. He's worried about her. He can't get her to speak with him and that is unusual for him. If we can't get her to speak with us, then it is really going to seem that she was involved in this somehow."

"And we know that she isn't. Someone is trying to frame her." Andrew leaned forward. "We're praying for you, Toryn, and for Slaney. Somehow, we'll get this figured out. Bill has taken an interest in it and is working with Aidan on it. Somehow he discovered that she had lived in Elmton at some point." Andrew referred to Bill Buckley, the lead detective on his force, and a very good personal friend.

"And we'll hear from Caleb Logan, the chief from Riverville, I have no doubt." Toryn sighed, a hand rubbing at his chest. It was sorer than he thought it should be. He just didn't want to say anything to anyone.

"How are you feeling?" Phoebe had appeared and reached to carefully hug the man she considered a cousin even though it had been proven that he wasn't. Phoebe had been kidnapped as a child by people who had kept her isolated for years. Toryn had been her one touch with reality. None of the relatives to the couple who had kept Phoebe hidden from her true family for years would even contact them in prison. Instead they stood behind Phoebe.

"Not great, Phoebe." Toryn knew better than to gloss over his health with Phoebe. "You would be a good one to speak with Slaney."

"And I will. But only with her permission and when she is ready to speak with me." Phoebe stood with a hand on Toryn's shoulder. "We're praying for you, Toryn. God is in control, even though it seems as if He's not."

"I know that He is. It's just sometimes hard to see it." Toryn was thoughtful, grateful for praying friends but more grateful that God was in control and that He was the Great Physician.

Chapter 10

Walking towards Slaney that afternoon, Daci studied her new friend. She was hiding, Daci decided. She had seen it too many times over the years.

"Slaney? What can we do for you?" Daci curled up at the opposite end of the couch, a grin on her face as Slaney stared at her. "We all want to do that. All of Don's team's ladies want to meet with you just to pray for you."

"They would do that?" Slaney was used to going through life on her own. She didn't know what to think.

"They would. None of us are working tomorrow. Are you?"

Slaney shrugged. She didn't want to admit that she wrote true crime columns under an alias and that these columns had been picked up by many newspapers, both print and on line. She was ahead with her columns but was deep in research for another true crime book.

"I can be. I'm doing some research for something but I can do that at any time." Slaney sighed, knowing that at some time she would need to come clean with her work.

"You don't have to tell us what you do. That doesn't matter. As long as it's legal and above board, we're fine with not knowing. Now, Toryn and Aidan will continue to probe until they find out." Daci laughed at the face that Slaney pulled.

"I know that they will. Unfortunately, I can't tell them. I have hidden my work to such an extent that they would only find out through my lawyer. I just don't want anyone to know. There are lives at stake because of what I do." She didn't hear Don as he approached and then found a chair where he could watch her.

"But it is legal what you do?" Don's voice had her head shooting around as she discovered him in the room.

"It is, Don. It is." She sighed. "I guess that I do need to come clean about my life. But Toryn and Aidan need to hear it as well."

"We'll get together with them tomorrow. Take tonight just to get your thoughts sorted out. Do you want your lawyer there?" He waited patiently for her to speak.

"Not tomorrow. I won't say anything past when I finished university. I can't until I speak with them." Slaney blinked, her eyes thoughtful. "I have worked too hard to cover what I do and to protect myself. I have had to do that." Her thoughts drifted off to her childhood and she forgot about the two in the room with her.

Daci was on her feet at last, heading for her kitchen. Whether or not they felt like eating, they needed to. Don nodded as she laid a hand on his shoulder, knowing that Delanie was around somewhere. He thanked God for the lady who shared his life, a helpmeet God had provided for him.

Delanie turned as Don approached her a while later to be wrapped in his arms. She hugged him before she stepped back.

"What can we do for her, Don?" Delanie kept her voice low, not sure where Slaney was.

"Pray for her. She wants to meet with Toryn and Aidan but only to discuss her life up to when she finished university. She is refusing to discuss her life or work after that."

"She's afraid, Don, deeply afraid. And now she is worried for anyone who is in contact with her. That makes me think that there is a crime involved somehow." Delanie stepped away. "I looked up her name. This is what I found." She looked past Don to find Slaney standing there. "Slaney?"

Slaney reached for the papers and walked away. She could not be angry with Delanie. Delanie had done what she would have done. Slaney walked out of the house to find a seat outside. She didn't care that it was dull and that rain was threatening. It just matched her mood.

Delanie found her a while later and sat near her, uncertain as to her welcome. Slaney's head turned to watch her.

"It's okay, Delanie. I'll give it back after I talk to Toryn and Aidan. They need to know first." Slaney blinked back tears. It still hurt after all those years.

"I'm sorry, Slaney. I wish that your life had been different."

"It is what it is. I can't change it. God was there for me, Delanie. I can only walk forward with His help. That's what I have always done."

Delanie nodded and then turned the conversation to other topics, including Toryn. He was a good friend to Don and she had come to appreciate the man behind the badge.

Toryn looked up the next day, hearing Aidan's voice. He was not feeling the best that morning. His mother had been pushing him to call the surgeon but he had been putting it off. Toryn knew that he would need to and soon.

Aidan dropped his portfolio on the table in front of the couch, assessing his friend. Don had called and advised him that Slaney was on her way. She wanted to talk with both Toryn and himself. And that he should be prepared for a horror of a story. No, he didn't know the details, but Slaney had dropped enough hints for him to know that it would be devastating for his friend to hear.

Slaney stepped into Tavin's house, finding Toria waiting for her. Toria simply swept her into a hug, praying for the young lady who seemed to mean so much to her son. Slaney hugged her back, not having felt a mother's hug in so many years.

Toria stood back at last, watching as Slaney swiped at her face. Her heart was breaking for the young lady standing in front of her.

"Toryn's in the living room, Slaney. So is Aidan." Toria made a move to walk away, stopping as Slaney clutched at her arm. "Slaney?"

“You need to hear this too. Is Tavin here?”

“No, he’s at an appointment.” Toria’s arm was around Slaney, turning her towards the living room. She nodded at Don who stood just inside the door. Toria knew that his team was around outside. It was a given as the younger people would have said.

Chapter 11

Slaney found a seat, somewhat reluctantly, beside Toryn, Toria sitting beside her. She refused to look at the two men, ashamed somewhat that it had come to this. She had always hidden her past, not wanting to be looked down on. Don found a seat in the room, just inside the door. Slaney had insisted that he be there. He had agreed, his heart breaking for his new friend all the while that he was praying for her.

Aidan simply began to pray for her and heard Toryn and Don picking up the petition. He didn't raise his head right away, feeling the presence of God in the room. That always happened, he decided, when Toryn prayed. He had a way of praying that brought them right to God's throne.

Looking up, Slaney didn't see censure on any of the faces of the people with her in the room. She drew in a deep breath, trying to steady her nerves and find the words that she needed. She felt Toryn's arm around her as he drew her close to him. His hug brought comfort, peace, and strength to her. She felt that now she could start her story.

"I need to apologize, Aidan. I won't talk about my life after university. I have worked too hard to protect myself and I won't do anything to change that. I will provide the name of my lawyer and you can speak with him. He is aware that you might need to." Slaney slumped against Toryn, not hearing his slight groan as she did so. She straightened back after a few seconds. "Where do I start?"

Aidan was watching her and nodded. She doesn't want to speak, he knew, but he needed her to talk with him, either there or in an interrogation room at the police department.

"Start with your parents, Slaney." Aidan reached for his notepad and pen and then instead reached for his laptop, knowing that he would need to make notes.

Nodding, Slaney shot a look up at Toryn, realizing for the first time that he was holding her. She frowned at him as she saw a look in his eyes that said that she was important to him.

"Okay. Dad was a reporter who was assigned to the crime beat in our town. He was good at it, finding information that the authorities could not. People trusted him. His name? Shane. Mom, Anna, stayed at home. They had decided that if they had any children, Mom would do that. I had a brother just two years younger than me. Shannon and I were close, more than most siblings. We did have our squabbles but no real fights. We were taught to pray through our differences with one another. That always worked.

"I was twelve when it happened. I heard a noise in the house and Dad shouting. I hid under my bed not knowing what was happening. I had taken my phone and called for help. The police officer who found me carried me out, just telling me to hide my eyes against him. I did. I think that I sensed something was really wrong but I had no idea what. He took me to an ambulance and then to the hospital. I wasn't harmed, not physically.

—

"A detective came to speak with me. I didn't understand why my parents hadn't come to find me." Slaney had to stop to control her emotions, taking with a soft thank you the facial tissues handed to her. "He told me that Dad, Mom, and Shannon were dead. Someone had broken into the house and killed them. They think that the man or men looked for me but the police response drove them away. They have never found the ones who did this. I had to go into foster care at that point." She waited for a moment to let the information sink in. Slaney found Toryn's arm tightening around her. "I have kept in contact with that department over the years but there has been no movement in the investigation.

"My foster family was wonderful. They were both police officers which is why I was placed there. It was a safety issue for me. They were Christians and that helped immensely. I obtained scholarships to go to university. I didn't feel as if it was safe for me to make friends there. I always felt as if I was being followed but I couldn't prove it. I moved towns frequently just to try and hide. I think those men who shot Toryn found me. I can't prove it. And I don't know that it was related to the shooting at the robbery."

Horror had moved across the faces of those listening to them. They had no idea that this is what her life had been like. It didn't surprise the three men that she was very protective of her life and that was why there was little information out there on her. She had had good advice with respect to that.

Aidan stared at his notes. He would be looking into that event and also contacting the detective who was on the case. He hated that she had been through this with no end in sight. Aidan frowned at Toryn who was watching him closely. They would speak, he knew.

"I can't add anything more, Aidan." Slaney handed over a piece of paper. "This is the detective to whom I speak every few months. And no, I will not tell you what my work is. I can't." She was on her feet, running from the room. Don followed her, tucking her into his truck and then heading away with her to Daci's home. He knew that his team was surrounding them.

Toryn's head dropped as Slaney moved rapidly away from him. He had to let her go. He would find her later, he knew.

Aidan rose at least, heading for his office. He had been shaken by what Slaney had said and needed to do some research on her. He turned as he heard Lyle's voice.

"Aidan?" Lyle frowned at his detective. "You look disturbed."

"I am." Aidan pointed at his office. "We need to talk, Lyle. Slaney has opened up about her early life and why it is so hard to find out anything about her." Aidan brought Lyle up to date on what Slaney had shared.

Lyle was shocked, to put it mildly. He stared at Aidan who simply nodded.

"I see. I wonder.." Lyle's voice died away for a moment. "The robbery? I wonder if that was done to bring Slaney out into the open. Her father's occupation would be known if someone was following her for years. She may well be an investigative reporter but not telling anyone."

"That is what she has stated. She will not say what she does. I don't know what it is but we can certainly look at that angle." Aidan was saddened, knowing that Slaney had been deprived of her family just at a time when she needed them most. "She didn't say anything about other family members."

"She didn't? We have a consultant, don't we, who does family trees for law enforcement?" Lyle was working through what investigations would need to be started. This had just compounded the investigation.

"Kat. One of Abe's team member's wives. I'll reach out to her. And to Emma." Aidan sighed. This is not how the day was to have gone.

"On another note, how is Toryn?" Lyle had intended to make his way over to see Toryn the day before but had not made it.

"He's hurting, Lyle. His colour is still off. This with Slaney? It's weighing heavily on him seeing as he did know her from university. And not being able to be part of the investigations? That is weighing even heavier. He's hurting for our people."

"He is. I need to speak with Aaron. Even though Toryn is off on sick leave, we need to keep him up to date on as much as we can." Lyle looked down for a moment. "May has been preparing a list daily of where each investigation stands. She told me that she had to. Toryn would ask for it at some point."

—

"And she's totally correct. Why don't you head over there while I contact both Kat and Emma." Aidan was not sure if he should but as an investigator, he felt that he had to. "And then there's Darcy. She'll do a profile for us." Darcy was the wife of a fellow officer from Riverville, a retired forensics psychologist who still stepped in to help friends.

Slaney looked up from her research late that afternoon. She had immersed herself into it once Don had dropped her off. Daci had already left her home for work by the time that Slaney was back. She had a new column to write but was not really interested in it.

Turning instead to the folder that she had saved to her laptop, she opened it, praying for peace and answers. Over the years, she had gone back over her father's articles, one in particular staying with her. She frowned. It was beginning to sound all too familiar. And that scared her more than she had ever felt fear in her life.

On her feet, she paced the sunroom, hearing voices from the kitchen. Slaney sighed. She needed to talk with someone. The thing was that the only one she wanted to speak with was Toryn. And she didn't think that she could burden him at this point.

Daci looked around as Slaney approached, a huge smile on her face. She waved at the ladies who had gathered.

"These are our ladies, Slaney. They are married to Don's team members. You have met Delanie."

"I have. Please, introduce me." She hesitated for a moment. "I'm sorry. I really don't have that many social skills. I have had to stay in hiding for most of my life."

"You have?" Delanie reached to hug her. "Sound like a mystery that we can sink our teeth into."

"It may be. I have come to the conclusion that I am tired of running and hiding. I need to take back my life." Slaney was determined to do just that, starting with meeting with these ladies.

"And we will certainly help you. I'm Payten. Paul is my husband. Let me introduce you to the others. This is Thomas' Taran, Caleb's Cullea, Joshua's Jincy, and Mark's McKala. We'll work with you, if you'll let us."

"That would help." Slaney sighed. "And I just know that Toryn will want to be involved. How do I let him when he's injured"

Taran was shaking her head. She knew Toryn only too well, she decided.

"It's not going to be an option, Slaney. He'll work on it on his own and figure it out eventually. However, it will stress him that you're not sharing with him. He's interested in you. I hear from Toria that Toryn is asking every day if you are safe and sound." She grinned at the look on Slaney's face.

"And he has never dated, Slaney." Cullea reached to hug Slaney. "To have him asking about you like this? It's not the Toryn we know. This goes beyond you just being a victim of crime. It's personal with him."

Slaney stared at Cullea and then around at the other ladies, finding them nodding. She watched as Daci moved to answer her door, hearing other female voices. She felt overwhelmed for a few moments, with Jincy moving in to hug her and pray for her.

"Ladies. We have company. Slaney, this is Emma, Kataleen or Kat as she prefers, and Darcy. All the way from Riverville to spend time with us." Daci knew why the three ladies had appeared or thought that she did. Someone had reached out to them. "Emma has a business where she finds people and information that no one else can. Kat has a family tree program that she uses to help catch criminals. And Darcy is a retired forensics psychologist who does profiles for her friends of whoever it is that's after them. But first, ladies, let's eat. It was warm enough today that I picked up cold meat and salads. There's enough for all."

Kat grinned as she held up a bag.

"And Rylee sent some of her goodies from her bakeshop. She wanted to come but she and Dave had a meeting tonight that she could not get out of."

An hour later, Slaney sat back, flushed with laughter. She had needed this, she decided, not having realized just how isolated her own life had been. Slaney had made that decision after consultation with her lawyer and law enforcement when she became an adult. They had felt that it had been necessary as she was the only one left who might know who had murdered her family.

Emma watched Slaney over the course of the time that they spent together. She was worried about her friend, Toryn, and this lady who seemed to have become involved in his life. She had not been able to find out much about Slaney and that both puzzled and concerned her. Emma resolved to speak with Slaney at some point that night if the opportunity presented itself.

Slaney looked around late that night. She felt welcomed by the ladies who had taken her to their hearts and just opened up their group to include her. Emma, Kat, and Darcy had done the same. She had been grateful for that. Slaney had not had that companionship during the years since she had become an adult. No one had felt it would be safe for her. She made the determination at that point that she had hidden herself enough. Slaney was ready to take her life and had said as much. The ladies had laughed at the way she had said it and then had agreed with her. Their plans for her to do that had been outrageous, causing much laughter but leaving Slaney feeling that she had friends that would stand by her.

Daci came looking for Slaney, watching her friend. She had observed the release that had happened that night with Slaney and was grateful that God had answered their prayers. Only it made it much more difficult for her. And that meant more danger for Slaney and also Toryn. Daci knew her friend would not walk away from Slaney.

"Slaney? What are your plans for tomorrow? It's Saturday." Daci grinned at her.

"My plans? I don't know that I have any. Why?"

"Because we're going to start putting your plans into play. Let's go out for brunch and do some

———

shopping. Then, we'll stop by and see Toryn. He'll be looking for you to do that."

"I don't understand why." Slaney stared at her hands which she had clasped together in her lap. She blinked as she looked at Daci. "He said that he loved me and then kissed my hand. He didn't mean that. He was just rousing when he said that."

Daci gave a small smile. She knew Toryn well enough to know that he just didn't say those words without meaning them.

"He meant that, Slaney. Toryn does not say anything that he does not mean. If he said that, then he spoke the truth."

Slaney stared at her friend, hope rising in her heart that Toryn did mean that but her mind telling her that it wasn't true.

Saturday found Slaney and Daci wandering through the downtown area. Slaney felt uncomfortable at doing that but Daci had dragged her from the house and to the downtown area.

"Daci? Just what are we planning on doing?" Slaney frowned as Daci laughed at her, Don appearing behind his sister.

"To get you out and about. That is what we're doing. If Toryn was well enough, he would be out here with you." Don looked past him to see Toryn standing there. "Toryn? Are you supposed to be here?"

Toryn shrugged. He was still somewhat shaky on his feet but when he heard of Slaney's plans for the day, he just had to be there. He just didn't think it through all that well.

"Don? Are we just going to stand here or are we heading for Ben's beside us?" Daci's voice finally broke through the silence. She watched as Toryn studied Slaney and Slaney studied him in return. She shared a somewhat amused look with Don.

"Ben's, I think." Toryn reached for Slaney's hand and tugged her with him into the diner, waving at Ben as he did so. He found a booth at the back and tucked Slaney onto a seat before he slid in beside her.

Slaney just stared at Toryn, shocked at how he had just maneuvered her to a seat. Her mouth opened and closed as she saw the amusement that lurked in his eyes.

"Toryn?" Ben walked up to them, menus in his hands. "Should you be here?"

Toryn shrugged, his eyes carefully searching the diner. It was a force of habit with him. He didn't see anyone that stood out but he felt the eyes watching him. The tingle on the back of his neck told him that someone was monitoring them. Don nodded at him as he glanced at him.

"I don't know that I should be, Ben, but I can't stay at home." Toryn handed a menu to Slaney. "You know my usual. What would you like, Slaney?"

Slaney shrugged. Eating out was not something that she had done frequently. If she wanted something from a restaurant, she just had take-out. She could see that Toryn was determined that he was going to change that for her. Slaney looked around, uncomfortable at being out in the open. She had hidden for so long that she wasn't sure about the proper protocol to follow any more.

The four lingered over their meals, conversation light between them. Toryn rose at last, his hand reaching for Slaney's as they walked from the diner. He looked around, not seeing anyone who stood out but he knew that someone was there.

"Toryn? You need to be resting." Slaney tried to get him to go home.

Only Toryn was not having any of that. Not right at the moment, anyway. He shook his head at her before he turned to hear what Don was saying.

"Toryn? Let's get you home. And yes, Slaney can come too. You're shaky on your feet."

"Yeah, I guess that's what we need to do." He walked towards Don's truck, not seeing the look that Daci was giving him.

Tavin looked around as he heard the laughter that sounded through his home as the four younger people entered the house. He smiled. It was good to hear Toryn laughing again. Slaney was good for him, he decided.

Late that night, Slaney snuggled down under her covers, a smile on her face. Toryn had treated her as if she was the most important person in the world to him. Daci had hugged her as they walked into Daci's home and then disappeared.

Toryn paced his bedroom. He smiled as he thought back over the day. He could see Slaney's personality starting to peek through. Toryn was glad about that. He just worried about her. He would need to have a long talk with Aidan and that would happen on Monday. He wanted to know where the investigations stood. Somehow, Toryn had become convinced that the robbery was directly related to Slaney and was an attempt to draw her out into the open. He wanted to know how they had found her. And he also wanted to know what she did for work. Slaney had just refused to tell him

Neither of the couple heard the motions outside of the homes where they were. Daci did and was on her feet, searching her video feed. She watched the men as they crept around her house but didn't get close. She sighed. Now what? She would need to speak with Don and she didn't want to do that. He would try to help but sometimes his help was not helpful.

Toryn was on his feet in the morning, feeling better. Being able to be out on Saturday had helped. He was feeling somewhat stronger and was determined to be in church that morning and to move back to his own home that afternoon. Toryn expected a fight from his mother and was surprised when she simply told him that she had shopped for him.

Toryn approached the church building, not sure what to expect. He found some of Don's men moving in around him even as officers did the same. He was being protected and wasn't sure what to expect. He searched for Slaney and headed her way, surprising her by hugging her and then turning her to find a seat at the back of the church.

That evening, Slaney walked through Daci's home, knowing that she was needing to be on her own. She wasn't sure what she wanted to do but she definitely felt that she was needing to be on her own as grateful as she was to Daci.

Don nodded the next morning as Slaney approached him. He had fully expected her decision.

"Where do you want to live?" Don's question stopped Slaney who spun to face him.

"I need a house that is not too close to anyone else. Whoever is after me? They won't stop until they reach me. And it won't matter to them if someone gets in their way. I need Toryn to stay away from me."

Don began to laugh, causing Slaney to glare at him.

"It's okay, Slaney. I know of a house that would suit you. We've used it in the past as a safe house so the security is good. And it is near the downtown area, which works for you. As to Toryn? He's not going anywhere too far from you, Slaney. We can all see that he is worried and concerned about you. There is also a tone in his voice when he says your name. None of us have ever heard that tone when he says a lady's name."

Chapter 14

Toryn walked into the department the next morning, albeit not with his usual quick step. He made it a point to stop and speak with each officer and civilian employee. It was who he was and what he did. He finally made it to his office and sank gratefully into his chair. His elbows hit his desktop as he dropped his head into his hands. His prayer was raising for his people and for the families. Toryn planned on visiting them the next day, his mother promising to be his driver.

Aidan stopped at Toryn's open door, surprised to see him. He entered and sat in front of the desk, his eyes on his friend. Toryn shouldn't be here, he knew, but he also acknowledged that he had to be.

Toryn looked up at last, his chin resting on his hands. He didn't say anything, just watched Aidan.

"You're not supposed to be here, Toryn." Aidan finally spoke.

"I know. I know that I'm not." Toryn sighed. "I know that I'm off on leave and am not supposed to be here. I have to, Aidan. I need to be there for our people."

"They know that you are there for them. They want you to take the time that you need to heal." Aidan looked sideways as he heard a noise and saw Aaron entering as well.

Aaron shook his head at Aidan, sharing his thoughts that Toryn shouldn't be there.

"Toryn?" Aaron's quiet voice brought Toryn's eyes to him. "What are you doing here?"

Toryn shrugged, not quite sure himself. He sighed. He knew better and was feeling worse every moment.

"I know, Aaron. Where do the investigations stand?"

"Not where we want them to, that's a given. We have no idea who the robbers were. There was no evidence found at all. And the surveillance tapes that we viewed do not give much information on them." Aaron was frustrated. "And that with you and Slaney? We're no further ahead with that. Aidan has spoken with the detective in her hometown and that detective is forwarding the file to us. We'll have it later today. Once we've gone over it, we'll speak with Slaney again." Aaron grew quiet for a moment. "It's hard to understand who would have done this. And does it connect to the robbery?"

"That's what has been puzzling me. How would it connect?" Toryn leaned back in his chair, a soft moan coming from him. "We don't know what Slaney does for a living, do we?"

"No, we don't. She's not sharing that. It can't be illegal, not knowing her." Aidan frowned for a moment. "I wonder."

Aaron looked at him and waited for him to continue.

"What do you wonder, Aidan?" Toryn spoke for Aaron as well.

"Her father was a reporter. Would she have taken up the same occupation?" Aidan was watching Toryn as he spoke.

Toryn nodded, that thought having already crossed his mind. He doubted that they would ever get an answer from her.

"Have you spoken with her lawyer?" Toryn was thinking through how to determine just what she did without asking her directly.

"I have." Aidan was frustrated with that. "He has refused to tell us what she does. And we can't force him."

"No, we can't." Toryn sighed as he shoved himself to his feet. "Anything that I need to take care of, Aaron?"

"Just yourself." Aaron walked out with Toryn, finding Toria waiting for him.

"Mom?" Toryn turned to his mother as they drove away towards his home. "Has Slaney said anything about what she does?"

"No, she hasn't, son. I know that she does a lot of research but she hasn't said why. And I won't ask. She'll tell us when she trusts us enough to do so. She has not been able to live a life that was safe for her. And she has that mystery in her life that doesn't seem to be solvable."

"I know, Mom. I worry about her. I am afraid that we won't solve what's going on before she is seriously injured or killed."

—

"You're doing God's work, son. And I understand why. She is a lady you're interested in getting to know better. You've never been in that position before." Toria glanced at her son as she pulled to a stop in his driveway. "Your dad and I are praying for you, son. You know that. We are also praying for Slaney. We don't know what the future holds. Only God does. It is hard to trust Him in situations such as this. That's where our faith comes in."

Toryn nodded, knowing that she was correct. All he could do was to be there for Slaney and wrap her in both prayer and his arms when he could. He wanted to run and find her but didn't. He needed to let her approach him as she would. Toryn knew that he would stand beside her.

Slaney looked up from her laptop and then stretched. She had been working away for hours, she decided. Don watched her for a moment, seeing the strain that she was trying hard to hide. He needed to get her together with Toryn at some point. They didn't have a team in for security training that week and he nodded. Tomorrow, he would bring Toryn out here and meet with his team to decide what they could do.

Looking at her email, Slaney sighed. Emma and Kat had both sent emails. She didn't want to look at them right now. She would look at them tomorrow. On her feet, Slaney headed for her bedroom, dropping her laptop on the dresser before she sank onto the bed. Her head was bowed as she prayed for herself and for Toryn. She turned as she heard a tap at her door.

Cullea entered as Slaney looked around. She and Caleb had dropped in not that long ago, bringing a

___

meal for them. She sat beside Slaney, an arm out to hug her.

"Slaney? Are you up for a meal?"

"You know? I think that I am. I want this over and I don't know how to do that." Slaney was on her feet, joining Cullea as she laughed and then linked arms with her, heading them for the kitchen.

The two men looked around before Don headed for the door. He stared at Toryn standing there and then waved at Tavin as he backed his car out.

"Should you be here?" Don had a grin on his face.

Toryn grinned in response. No, he knew that he should not be there. But this is where Slaney was and he wanted to be near that lady. She helped him feel at peace and not as restless.

Slaney felt arms hugging her from behind and leaned back. It had to be Toryn, she decided. He was the only one who would do that. And she was not about to tell him to stop.

Chapter 15

Toryn studied Slaney carefully that night. She was freer in how she spoke and her laughter was more spontaneous. He was glad. He could see God working in her life. Slaney in turn was observing Toryn. He was looking somewhat better, she decided.

"Slaney?" Toryn approached her near the end of the evening. "I am worried about you."

"Don't do God's work for Him. I know that you are worried. But it is what my life is." She bit at her lip. "Emma and Kat sent me some information. I just don't want to read it."

"I would be willing to help you with that. Can we get together tomorrow?" Toryn saw Don hesitate before he walked into the room. "Don can bring you to me or I can come to you."

"How be you come here?" Slaney sighed. This wasn't her home and here she had just asked Toryn to come to it.

"It's okay, Slaney. We can meet in the office. My team would like to help you with this. They worked on the adventures that each other had. And we have another team that would be willing to help. I understand that Andrew and Bill are heading this way tomorrow." Don grinned at her. "You'll have more help than you need, I can guarantee that. And if it involves your work, if you wish to share with us, we'll accept that. If you don't feel that you can, it's okay. We know that what you do is above board." Don walked away at that, leaving Slaney blinking rapidly to control the tears that threatened to spill over.

"Slaney?" Toryn reached to hug her. "I'm off. Call me if you need me."

Slaney stared up at the tall, handsome man standing in front of her and made a decision. She handed him a book, a frown on his face as she did so before she walked away. Toryn stared after her and then at the book. He didn't recognize the author and wondered why she had handed it to him.

Don was waiting for him and looked down at the book.

"Slaney give you that?" At Toryn's nod, Don frowned. "Do you know the author?"

"No, I don't. I'll do some research but she gave it to me for a reason. She is trusting me with something and I don't want to do anything to break that trust. She doesn't trust easily."

Don had to agree with that. He had watched Toryn and Slaney that evening, seeing a connection between the two. All he could do was pray for them.

Early in the morning, Toryn set the book aside. It had been a true crime novel but it rang too true. He wondered at that. He knew without being told that names and situations had been changed but he was sure that it was Slaney's family. Is this what she did, he asked himself? He did some research on the author but found no information on him. The book itself had become a best seller and that did not surprise him. The details had been graphic and too true to life. It was also an unfinished story, just like Slaney's.

Slaney stared at the window where she could see the lightening of the darkness. Morning was coming. She had some decisions to make that would destroy the safety net she had managed to surround herself with. Slaney had spent some time the day before on a call with her lawyer. He had given her some good advice and offered to come and be there when she met with the detectives. She had gratefully accepted his offer and it was scheduled for the next day. Today, Slaney had to make it through without the men guessing what she did. She didn't want it out in the open.

Giving Toryn that novel had taken a lot from her. She was trusting him with a secret that she wasn't ready to share. She knew him well enough to know that he would guess that the novel was her life. But she also knew that he would not say anything without speaking with her. For that, she was grateful. She was becoming free from the shackles that had surrounded her most of her life. Slaney was breaking free and running towards life. Only, it was just so dangerous for her and anyone who got in the way. Slaney was running towards love and towards Toryn. She had come to know him well enough to know that he didn't say what he had without there being feelings there. She was beginning to care deeply for him, sensing God nudging her Toryn's way.

Toryn stood for a moment that morning and watched Slaney as she worked away on her laptop. She was writing, he decided, and wondered what crime

—

that she was writing about. He walked forward towards her, his socked feet barely making a sound. Toryn knew that she was aware that he had approached her, a quick glance from her telling him that. He simply sat near her and watched her concentrate on what she was working on.

"Toryn?" Slaney spoke at last, her eyes not raising from where she stared at the laptop.

"Slaney? Are you okay?" Toryn had been very worried about his friend or his lady as he now thought of her.

Slaney shrugged. She had no idea how to feel. And that worried her. She should be feeling something. Her emotions were all over the place and she just could not get a clear sense of what she was feeling.

"I don't know any more, Toryn. I really don't know. How do I get through this?" She looked up at last, a questioning look in her eyes.

"That's not unusual. You're going through a lot right now. The past is coming up again and you need to deal with the emotions that you felt as a child and what you feel now about it. I want to help you." Toryn reached to hug her, drawing her away from her laptop. Her hand closed the top on it and then she was hugging Toryn back.

"Toryn? You have questions." Slaney sighed to herself.

"I do. I read the novel. I know that it's your life. I won't tell anyone." Toryn simply held his lady as her emotions finally broke and she sobbed, huge heartbroken sobs. His voice whispered prayers and Bible verses to help her.

Don paused as he saw Toryn and Slaney and then backed away. He nodded towards the conference room and his team walked that way. Their ladies were with them, wanting to help solve whatever it was that Toryn and Slaney were facing. It would only get worse for the couple, they all knew.

"Don?" Caleb paused beside him. "What all do we actually know?"

Don shrugged. He knew what Caleb was asking and had no answer for him.

"I'm not sure. I know that Emma and Kat have been in touch with Slaney. Slaney mentioned that she had received emails from them. She wants to go over them with us. I suspect that everything has just overwhelmed her like a tsunami. She has to break at some point. Thank God that Toryn is there."

Caleb grinned for a moment, the whole team certain that Toryn had found his lady. They had not gotten to know Slaney very well but their ladies were adamant that this was the case.

Chapter 16

Slaney took the tissues handed to her and swiped at her face. She very seldom broke down as she just had. Her emotions were always kept rigidly in check. Somehow, Toryn had climbed the high wall that they were behind and had begun to break down that said wall, brick by brick. God had spoken to her through Toryn's care and she realized that what she had gone through had made her into the lady that she was. And God had also told her that it was time to let go and let Him work it all out and in doing that to heal her. She reached out to touch the hem of the garment and found solace and peace starting to work in her heart.

Toryn didn't move, his arms around his lady. He just continued to quote the verses that were needed. Afterwards, neither one of them could say one of the verses that he quoted. That didn't matter. God had used Toryn to reach out to Slaney.

"Slaney?" Toryn finally spoke, his eyes on the doorway to the office, seeing Thomas hovering there. Thomas was the paramedic on Don's team and was greatly worried about Slaney.

"Toryn?" Slaney studied him, seeing a look in his eyes that gave her hope that he was not disgusted with her. "How are you feeling?"

Toryn shrugged. He was feeling better to some degree. But how he was feeling was not the issue here, he decided. Slaney was. He wanted to make it all better for her but he couldn't. No matter how much

Aidan was searching into the two investigations, neither was moving forward to any great degree. And that worried Toryn. There should be something that could help. They just hadn't found that one piece of information to do just that.

"I'm okay, Slaney. I'm worried about you, though."

Slaney shoved away from him, heading for the door and then the washroom. She needed to find some hot water and wash away the remnants of her tears. Toryn rose and watched her, moving to the doorway to do to.

Thomas stood beside Toryn, a hand resting on Toryn's shoulder. He watched Slaney disappear and then turned to Toryn. He sighed. Toryn was in love, he decided, and didn't know how to proceed. Suffering a life-threatening injury was part of Toryn's hesitation, Thomas knew, but there was also the mystery surrounding Slaney. Depending on what it was, it could impact Toryn's position as police chief. They needed to solve this and solve it soon.

"Toryn? Are you or Slaney receiving anything that normally comes?"

"I haven't been. I don't know about Slaney. If she has, she's not said anything. And Daci has not said anything."

"And Daci would, that's a given." Thomas walked away, finding Taran waiting for him. He hugged his wife before he turned her back into the conference room.

Slaney slowly approached Toryn. She looked horrible, she decided, not realizing that Toryn thought of her as the most beautiful lady in the world. He simply opened his arms to hug her before he prayed for her. She relaxed against him.

"Ready to get to work?" Toryn waited until she nodded. "We will not pry or push you, Slaney. We want this over for you. And we will work with you. Your memories are going to rush out and overwhelm you."

"I know. That scares me." Slaney hesitated before she found a seat beside Payten, not surprised that Payten hugged her. Payten had spent time with her the day before. She had lost her parents in a house fire and Slaney was grateful for the support that lady was giving her.

Don bowed his head, knowing that they needed that time spent before God. God would be the One leading in their work that day. He would be the One providing the answers for them. Aidan slipped into a chair, his own head bowing as he joined in the prayer.

Don watched Slaney closely, waiting for her to speak. What they did now and in the near future would depend on her leading in the next few moments. He knew that the others in the room were watching her and waiting on her to make a movement.

Slaney sighed to herself, swallowed hard, and then reached for her laptop. She had printed off the emails from Emma and Kat, enough copies for each one. Don had insisted on that when she had balked at doing that.

"Okay. I have emails for all of you. Emma and Kat have sent on information. If you would read through them and then tell me what you think. I know what I think it says. I just need someone who doesn't know me well to look at it." Slaney began to pace in the hallway, Toryn's eyes following her before he turned back to the material.

Toryn was sore and tired and wanted nothing better than to go home and sleep. He would not do that. His lady needed him and he would not desert her, at least as long as he was able to.

Aidan reached for his copy of the material. Emma had already reached out to him, sending him on what she felt that she could. She had warned him that it was not pretty. He didn't expect it to be.

There was silence in the room except for the rustle of turning pages and the odd scratching noise from a pen. The ladies looked horrified at times whereas the men's faces grew increasingly grimmer. None of them could understand how Slaney had survived. They just didn't know who was behind it or what else that she had suffered and not be upfront about it with them.

Cullea was on her feet at last, heading to find Slaney. Slaney stared at her for a moment, shame and devastation on her face. Cullea shook her head and linked an arm with Slaney. She just paced with her friend. Slaney needed this support and Cullea was willing to give it. Words were not necessary between the ladies.

—

Aidan looked over at Toryn at last, seeing Toryn just sitting and staring at his notes. He moved to the chair beside his chief, waiting for Toryn to speak.

"This is brutal, Toryn." Aidan finally broke the silence in the room.

"It is. There's a lot more that she has not said. She's buried it too deep for it to just surface. And I'm afraid that once it does start to surface, she'll run from us in order to protect us." Toryn shifted restlessly. He had been sitting upright for too long and his muscles were protesting.

"She will. It's up to us to stop her. And we need to keep her presence here as quiet as we can. We have not released her name to the media. If any one of the reporters knows, they are not saying. Having had her father be a reporter is helping. There is a brotherhood there that is protecting her. The publishers have come to Aaron and let him know that they will not do anything to harm her or the investigation. We have not had to ask that of them."

"They will do that. They've done it before. I just didn't expect it to affect me." Toryn rubbed at his face. "How do we help her, Aidan?"

"That's a good question, Toryn." Joshua had turned to the two men. "We have this information. We have not been able to find anything on Slaney in our own research. We understand why. It just makes it more difficult."

"It does. And Slaney is not ready yet to tell us everything." Toryn's eyes locked with Slaney as she stood in the hallway watching him. A question was in her eyes and he shook his head slightly. She relaxed, knowing that Toryn would not betray her trust.

Chapter 17

Toryn tossed restlessly that night. He was unable to get to sleep and that bothered him. His thoughts were on Slaney and what they could do for her. Toryn had read the message in her eyes that afternoon, confirmation that the novel was her life. He prayed for her, not sure how to pray but knowing that God would hear his fumbling prayers.

His head raising, Toryn threw back the covers and pulled on his jeans. He had heard a sound outside and needed to investigate. He carefully opened the back door and peeked out, a large flashlight in his hands. It would serve as a weapon if he needed it. Toryn walked around his house and then through the yards, not seeing anything that was out of place. He just didn't see the men standing near the large oak tree in his front yard. The two men exchanged a look before they walked away, heading for the car that they had parked down the road. They drove off, knowing that they would be back at some point. Their employer would demand that of them.

Toryn slept at last, the sleep of pain and exhaustion. It was late when he awoke to the knocking at his front door. He stumbled that way, opening the door to find Aaron and Lyle standing there, grim looks on their faces.

"Fellows?" Toryn walked away, heading to get dressed. He paused as he reached for a clean T-shirt. Something had happened to bring them there. Aaron would not approach him unless it was urgent.

Aaron turned from the countertop. He had gone ahead and made the coffee for them all. Lyle was pacing, disturbed at what they had been told. Neither man knew how to talk to Toryn. Toryn would want to walk back into the office and that was not an option.

Toryn poured his mug of coffee and eyed the two men. Something had happened, he knew, and that was something major for them to be there.

"Okay, Aaron? Lyle? What happened? And don't tell me that nothing did."

"There has been a development in your shooting. We've gone back over the security feeds. They were following Slaney but didn't make a move on her. We've tracked them along the street. We also pulled the video feeds from the stores. They saw you and then started chasing Slaney towards you. It seems as if you were the target."

Toryn sat back, his face paling in shock at their words. He shook his head. That was not possible.

"Who?" He had to swallow hard before he spoke.

"We have their names at last." Aaron gave the names, seeing the look on Toryn's face. "Yes, them. We have the arrest warrants that we need and are moving in on them." Aaron was on his feet to take a phone call. Lyle was sitting where he could see Aaron's face. He didn't like the look that crossed the deputy chief's face.

Toryn was on his feet, watching Aaron closely. He read him correctly, he decided, and that reading said that the men were dead.

"Aaron?" Toryn spoke as Aaron tucked away his phone.

"The detectives found them, Toryn. They were both shot, execution style. From what we discovered, the men who shot you were responsible for setting up the robbery."

Toryn nodded. That was about what he had expected to hear. He paced away and then back towards the two men, sitting at last. Toryn rubbed at his face, knowing that this had just set back the investigation.

"Okay. It's about what I expected to hear. Lyle?" Toryn turned to the lead detective.

Lyle was on his feet, knowing that he had to head for the murder scene.

"I'll be in touch, Toryn." He was away before Toryn could respond.

Aaron watched Toryn before he prayed for his chief. This had certainly set back the investigations. They had hoped to find out who was behind the men but that would now take a lot of legwork and investigation.

"Toryn? What can I do for you?" Aaron's quiet question eventually broke through the silence in the room.

Toryn shrugged, his eyes on the window across from where he was sitting. He had no idea what to say.

"I don't know, Aaron. I really don't know. This is not going well, I must say."

"It is not. And we'll need to talk with Slaney. Where is she?"

"I have no idea. She was meeting with her lawyer this morning. And then I think she said something about heading this way." Toryn was on his feet as the doorbell rang. He opened it to find Slaney standing there, a man in his fifties standing beside her. "Slaney?"

Slaney gave a sniff and then moved into Toryn's space and his hug. He simply hugged her and then moved them backwards so that the door could be closed. He eyed the man before his eyes narrowed.

"You must be Slaney's attorney." Toryn's one hand went out to shake the man's extended one.

"I am. I am James Cheevers. Slaney needs to speak with you." James frowned. "You have company."

"My deputy chief. If it's okay with Slaney, I would like him to sit in on the meeting." He felt Slaney's head nodding against him. "Okay. How be we head into my office?"

Toryn watched as Slaney moved that way, greeting Aaron as she did so. He turned to the kitchen to make fresh coffee, knowing that it would be needed. James moved with him, his briefcase set down on the table as he asked what he could do to help him.

Turning his head, Toryn stared towards the hallway before he turned back to James.

—

"James? How is she?" Toryn turned to the tray that he had prepared, not quite sure how he was going to carry it. It was a little too heavy for him to pick up.

James had been watching Toryn and simply reached for the tray. He pondered the question that Toryn had asked. He knew Slaney well, having been a good friend of her parents.

"She's hurting, Toryn. All this is bringing back up emotions that she buried and never dealt with because of her age when it happened. As you are aware, we put her into a foster home where she could be protected. This was done privately. She had no family that could take her in. When she turned eighteen, we tightened up her life and kept it as secret as much as we could. She never rebelled against the restraints. That is, until now. Meeting you once more? She is fighting to be free of the restrictions. She has seen your friends and their lives and wants that for herself. She is looking to you for guidance and yes, love, which is something that she has never done in the past." James said no more, not willing to break Slaney's trust in him.

Chapter 18

Slaney shifted restlessly as she waited for one of the men to speak. She didn't look up as Toryn sat beside her. His arm was around her, tucking her close to him. Slaney leaned against him, drawing strength from him. God was showing her the character of the man who had stated that he loved her. And she was willing to find that out. He was supporting her without condemning her and that was not something that she had expected, not at all.

Aaron studied the couple and then turned to James, finding James with his eyes intent on Toryn. He wondered what James was thinking but knew that a good lawyer never gave anything away.

"Slaney?" Aaron saw Slaney jump before she looked at him. "You're here with your lawyer. What do you have to say? And do you want Aidan here?"

"I think we need him here. He's the investigator, isn't he?"

Aaron nodded before he was on his feet and heading for the door. He opened it to find Aidan standing there.

"Aidan?"

"Lyle sent me. We need to talk, Aaron, and talk with Toryn." Aidan frowned at Aaron. "Who all is here?"

"Slaney and her lawyer. I was just about to call you. Slaney is about to talk and we need you here as you're the investigator." Aaron pointed towards the office. "We're in there."

Aidan nodded, detouring through the kitchen to grab himself a mug of coffee. He then found a seat in the office, nodding at James. James had been in his office that morning before he met with Slaney. He provided what information that he could and then stated that Aidan would need to speak with Slaney. He could just not guarantee that Slaney would speak with Aidan. It might take many conversations between the investigator and the victim.

Slaney looked up at last, her eyes taking in the men who were in the room. She kept her gaze on James, waiting for him to nod. She would not speak unless he did that. That was a signal that they had agreed to. She, however, would not tell all that they wanted to know. She would keep her writing secret. Slaney felt that she had to at this point.

"Slaney? What do you need or want to tell us?" Aidan spoke at last, knowing that she was hesitant to speak.

Slaney shrugged. She felt Toryn's arm tightly slightly around her and took that to understand that he would stand behind her and beside her no matter what she said.

"I'm not sure what to say. I am struggling with so many emotions right now and so many images. I'm not sure what is fact or fiction." Slaney turned to James. "James?"

James nodded. Slaney and he had talked at length that morning. She had asked him to speak for her if she was unable to. And apparently, she was unable to speak at this point.

"Toryn. Aaron. Aidan. Slaney and I had a long discussion this morning. There are some aspects of her life that she will not tell you. One of those is her occupation. She is not doing anything illegal but prefers that her livelihood remain hidden. That is for her safety." He stopped speaking for a moment, his eyes on Toryn. He knows, James decided. Somehow, Slaney has managed to tell him without telling him in words. "As to her early life? You are aware that she was placed privately into a foster home with police officers. They were carefully chosen and vetted from among the families that came forward to take her in. Adoption was never offered to her and she was well aware as to why. That is something that will be discussed at a later time. For now? What Slaney wants to offer you is what information that she has on her parents. That is what is needed at present." James handed over file folders to the three other men. "In these are the facts that you need. I understand that Emma Finlay is researching as well. She has reached out to me to ensure that she has the correct information. She has stated that she is forwarding information to Slaney and once Slaney has seen it, she will forward it to you.

"I can confirm that someone has been trying to track Slaney for years, since her parents and brother were murdered. They had not been able to. Until now. Toryn? I have confirmation from a source that someone recognized Slaney at the same time that you appeared. You are a target as well. I have that information as to why included in that packet. Slaney

—

has asked that you three read through the information outside of her presence and then speak to me. She wants it that way. As she is my client, I would agree with that."

Toryn had tilted his head to watch Slaney, seeing the fear that she was trying hard to hide. He would do just about anything, he knew, to protect her. He just wasn't sure that they could.

"We can do that." Aidan spoke for the men, his eyes on Toryn and then Slaney. He heard murmurs of agreement from the other two men.

James was on his feet at last, heading for the door, Aaron with him. They stood for a few moments, speaking with one another before they drove off separately.

Aidan rose and gathered up the mugs and carried the tray back through to the kitchen. He set another pot of coffee and then glanced at the clock before he reached for bread and sandwich fixings. He would prepare a meal for them and then spend some time in prayer with them. What James had told him that morning had disturbed him greatly. He had also heard from Lyle that the robbers were dead but that they were the ones who had shot Toryn. Aidan was still trying to understand that. He wasn't sure that he did.

Toryn watched as Aidan walked away. He waited for Slaney to speak but she didn't.

"Slaney? Are you okay?" He waited patiently for her to speak.

Slaney shrugged. She was not sure how to feel any more. Toryn made her feel safe and content and loved. She was puzzled by that.

"I don't know, Toryn. I really don't know any more. James gave you what I would let him. I really don't want my occupation out there. It's too dangerous." Slaney was sober as she spoke.

"It's okay, Slaney. God knows how you feel. He's there for you and will never ever leave you or forsake you. And I won't either, not if I can help it." Toryn's arm tightened around her as he dropped a kiss on the top of her head.

—

Chapter 19

Toryn walked Slaney up to Daci's home. He was driving again, which he was so thankful for. He hugged her, prayed for her, and then shut the door after her. Toryn stared up at the evening sky for a moment before he headed for his truck. He was exhausted but more emotionally spent than anything else. He walked down to his truck and drove away.

Not noticing the truck following him, Toryn headed for his home. He pulled into his garage with the door closing behind him. He sat for a moment, not heading into his home. He was puzzled by something but it wasn't clear what it was. He would ponder it and it would come to him at some point.

Slaney walked through Daci's home, heading for the bedroom that she was using. She felt safe there but she wanted her own place and privacy. She would start looking in the morning, she decided, reaching for her Bible. She needed some God-time and searched for all the verses that she could find on hope and peace. God was working in her heart, releasing it from the bonds that she had felt she needed to keep it under.

Daci turned the next morning. She was off for that day, taking some personal time that she had accrued. She watched Slaney as she moved through the house before she approached her.

"Slaney? You want your own place." Daci didn't ask a question, merely stated a fact.

"I do, Daci. I worry about bringing trouble to your home. And I know that I will."

"You might. But I know that you are restless. You've been trying to be quiet so that you don't disturb me. I appreciate that. Now, find your purse or whatever it is that you need. I know of some houses that would work." Daci grinned at her friend as she herded her out of the door and to her car. "One is really close to Toryn's. Like right next door>"

"Next door?" Slaney didn't know if she wanted that but was game to see it.

Walking through the small bungalow later that morning, Slaney felt as if she had come home. It was furnished which was what she had wanted. Daci watched her before she turned to the door. Toryn stood there, a frown on his face as he saw Daci. He had handed over keys to some of the rental properties that he had to Don the night before. He had asked no questions, knowing that Don sometimes needed to use one of his homes for a short term placement.

"Daci?" Toryn stepped into the house, seeing Slaney walking back towards him. "Slaney?"

"Toryn? I like this house. I just need to find the landlord and tell him that I'll take it." She frowned as Daci began to laugh and Toryn just grinned at her. "What did I say?"

"Toryn's the landlord, Slaney. And I guarantee that the rent will be really reasonable." Daci walked away, leaving Toryn and Slaney staring at one another.

"You're the landlord? Daci didn't tell me that." Slaney turned back to wander through the house. It suited her just right, she decided. God had provided this home for her, that much she knew.

Toryn grinned as he toed off his sneakers and then moved to follow Slaney. He would be very happy, he decided, to have her living next door. He didn't want her out of his sight but would not make any move to advance their friendship.

"Slaney?" Toryn's voice brought her back to stand facing him. "You're sure?"

"I am. How much is the rent?" She frowned at him as he grinned and shook his head. "Toryn? The rent? How much is it?" She was surprised as he wrapped her into a hug. "Toryn?"

"There's no rent. It's okay, Slaney. It's what I do for friends." Toryn stepped back. "Are you ready to move in today?"

Slaney spun in a circle, eager to set up her home in that house but still uncertain as to whether she should or not. Toryn's hand on her shoulder stopped her motions.

"Let's get you back to Daci's and packed up. You'll need to do a food run as well." Toryn grinned at the look on her face.

"Okay, I guess." Slaney reached for her purse, frowning it. There was something about a purse that troubled her. She just couldn't remember what it was.

—

"Slaney? You've remembered something." Toryn was certain that she had. He was just not certain that she would share with him.

"Something about a purse. I can't remember what though." Slaney shrugged it off, not realizing that it was something important.

Late that night, Toryn found his favourite chair on his back deck. He closed his eyes for a moment, thanking God for getting him through another day. The pain that he was in had lessened as his strength was returning. He had seen the surgeon that morning. That man was amazed at how well and quickly Toryn had healed. Toryn had shrugged, simply stating that God as the Great Physician was healing him. The surgeon had stared at him and then stated that he would be at Toryn's church that next Sunday. There had to be something there.

His attention turned to the house next door and his smile widened. He was content to have Slaney next door to him. That helped him to keep an eye on her. He laughed softly as he remembered the look on her face when Daci had told Slaney just who owned the house. Toryn was glad to help her. He was falling deeper in love with the lady but was well aware that the mystery surrounding her had to be solved before he moved forward with dating her.

Slaney stood in the darkness of her bedroom, staring out at the back yard. She had not expected to find a home that suited her so well. And to be next door to Toryn? That she was grateful for. Slaney was falling in love but didn't know quite what to do. She was hesitant to ask any questions of the ladies who were become fast friends of hers. Slaney turned at last and sought her rest. She planned on spending the next few days writing. No one but her lawyer knew that she was the author of some of the true crime columns that had become so very popular. She was almost through with the one that she was working on and would send it to her lawyer tomorrow. James had worked with her on every column that she had written, gladly becoming the go-between for her and the newspapers and now the digital sites. Slaney knew that at some point she would have to go public with her name but she wanted to keep that as private as she could for as long as she could. True crime had not been something that she wanted to write about. Her early life had done that. Well, and the fact that this was one way to honour her father.

Chapter 20

Late the next afternoon, Slaney set her phone to one side. She rose and stretched. James had been in touch, just asking how she was. He had received a call from one of the publishers who had asked to meet the author of the columns. That man had been less than happy when James had refused his request. The unspoken threat against James had been recorded. James had always recorded any call relating to Slaney. He had gone to court at one point just after she became an adult and obtained a court order to do so. James knew that he had to call Slaney but right at the moment, he had a client waiting and that had to come first. He shot off a quick email to Aidan, just letting him know what had happened.

Aidan sat back in his chair after reading James' email. Things were beginning to heat up for Slaney, he decided, and that meant Toryn would become more involved. He sighed. He would need to find Toryn at some point that day.

Slaney turned from her back door late that afternoon. She had just spent a long time on a call with James. To say that she was highly disturbed and afraid was an understatement. She had taken great steps with James' guidance to hide her identity where it related to her writing. Slaney refused any and all offers to speak. She just didn't want to be out in the open. Only somehow that didn't seem to be working out so well lately. Toryn was taking her out and about as were Daci and the other ladies. Her life was becoming more and more open. She was afraid that her writing would endanger them or worse end with their deaths. Slaney knew herself well enough to know that she would never forgive herself if anyone was hurt because of her.

Hearing the door bell, Slaney frowned. She was not expecting anyone that she knew of. Peeking out of the side window, she continued to frown. Aidan was here and he did not look happy at all. That worried her. Her life felt like it was spiralling out of control and all her careful work of staying hidden was breaking apart.

Aidan turned back to the door as Slaney opened it, stepping into the hallway. He frowned at her for a moment.

"Slaney? When did you move?" Aidan was not happy that she had moved and had not let him know.

"Yesterday. And it's Toryn's house so I'm fine." Slaney glared at him for a moment before she headed for the kitchen. "Have you eaten? I have a casserole in the oven that's ready. I am not prepared to answer any questions or discuss anything until I've eaten."

Aidan suppressed a grin. She was growing vocal, he decided, different from what she had been. That was good, he knew. Maybe at some point, she would speak with him.

"I have not. And I do need to speak with you and before you eat. I have another appointment to get to in thirty minutes." Aidan refused to back down from her, his face expressionless as she glared at him once more.

"I have no answers for whatever questions that you may have. James called you." Slaney sighed, knowing that James would have reached out in such a way to let Aidan know that she was threatened but not the actual reasons why.

"He did. You need to talk to me, Slaney. I can't protect you if I don't know why or who." Aidan's hand slapped on the tabletop, frustration evident.

Slaney jumped at the sound, her face turning white. Sounds like that brought back the sounds of the gunfire from the night her family had died. She swayed for a moment before she grasped at a chair back, her knuckles white from how tight she was holding on to the chair.

"I can't, Aidan. I can't tell you what I do for a living. It is legal. There are too many people who may be harmed if I tell you that." Slaney's voice was barely above a whisper. "And I have taken too many steps to hide my work. I won't do that." She pointed towards the door. "I think that you need to leave." Slaney's back was turned towards him.

Aidan hesitated, knowing that he really did need to know what she did for a living. Only that was not happening. He walked away, anger rising inside him for a moment before he sighed. He couldn't make her speak with him at this point. At some point, he would even if he had to arrest her and force her to speak. He felt strongly that what had happened to Toryn was directly related to Slaney. His steps paused as a thought crossed his mind. Or was it? Maybe they were reading it wrong, thinking that Slaney was the catalyst to what had happened. What if she had just been in the wrong place at the wrong time? Aidan sent off a quick text to Lyle to ask that very question.

Toryn walked towards his home late that night. He had been at his parents' for a meal. Tavin had studied his son and then asked him what was going on. Something had happened, he decided.

"Son? Something has happened, hasn't it?" Tavin was not one to pry into his son's life. This time, he felt that he had to.

"It has, Dad. Slaney moved into the house beside me, the one that I own. She's opening up to me. I have a good idea what she does for a living but I won't break her confidence in me." Toryn stared down at his hands, folded on the table in front of him. "I am worried about her. And we're not really much further ahead in the investigations. I want this over with. Their families deserve the answers that we don't have as yet."

Tavin nodded. He had been watching his son and the others on the force. There was something going on there that he didn't understand.

"And you think that you're the cause of it?" Tavin didn't wait for his son to respond. "I know you, son. That's how you feel. And while you can feel that way, until it is proven that you are or aren't, you will bear that burden. You are also bearing the burden for your people because you can't be there on a daily basis."

"That's true, Dad. I want to be there but can't be. Does that even make sense?" Toryn was sober, knowing that his father had pegged his feelings. He was just unsure how to proceed.

"What did the surgeon say?" Toria shared a look with Tavin, changing the subject.

"He's quite happy with my healing. I am healing faster than he thought. He feels that I can go back to desk work in a couple of weeks." Toryn grinned suddenly. "He's coming to church on Sunday. I told him that God was healing me this quickly."

"That's wonderful, son." Toria reached to hug him. "Sometimes, God will use us to reach others through the difficulties that we have faced. And He can and will use those types of circumstances to bring villains to justice. I just wish it had not been you."

"Me, too. We're still working through where the investigation is going. We're not sure now which one of us is the target."

"It could be you or it could be Slaney. Or it could be both of you." Tavin looked at Toryn, finding his son watching him closely as well. "We'll work it through. I hear that Emma and Abe are heading our way."

"They are. They want to meet with Slaney again." Toryn bit at his lip, a sign to his parents that he was unsure about something but wasn't ready to share anything with them.

Chapter 21

The next morning found Toryn staring out at the rain that was pouring down. Rain had been forecast but he had not expected it to be so heavy. His gaze raise to Slaney's home before he reached for his rain slicker and slipped into shoes. He moved rapidly across the lawn until he as on her back deck and tapping at it.

Slaney looked around from where she was sorting papers on the kitchen table. She frowned at the knock before she stepped to where she could see out of the door window. She sighed. Toryn just had to show up, didn't he? Opening the door, Slaney walked back to where she had been working.

"Slaney? Are you okay?" Toryn was worried about her without knowing why.

Slaney shrugged. Today had been a bad day for her. It was the anniversary of her family's deaths. This year, it was hitting harder than ever. Toryn was watching the emotions flickering across her face before he was across the room and holding her. His hug broke through the restraints that she was trying hard to hold onto and she broke down, sobbing as his arms tightened around it. It was coming to a head, she thought, and she just wanted it all over with.

Toryn just held her until her sobs stopped and then continued to hold the lady he loved. Slaney hugged him at last and then stepped back, refusing to look up at him as she moved away to find a damp cloth to scrub at her face. God was working in her life, opening the gates to the emotions that she had locked away for years.

"Slaney?" Toryn watched her closely still, not willing to walk away from her.

"It's okay, Toryn. It's been a bad day. This is the anniversary of their deaths. Usually I just ignore the day and go through it without thinking about what day it is. This year, that isn't working." She pointed to the papers on the table. "I've been going back through all the information that I have amassed over the years. I didn't know that I had gathered that much."

Toryn studied her and then turned to the table, picking up pile after pile and reading through them. He looked around, taking with a smile and a word of thanks the pad of paper and pen that Slaney handed him. He was lost in what he was doing, not seeing how Slaney was watching him before she glanced at the clock. They would need to eat soon and she just didn't feel like preparing anything. Toryn held out his phone, simply telling her to call Ben at the diner. He would bring them something to eat. And she didn't have to be specific as to what she asked for. His attention was still on what he was reading.

An hour later and with their meal completed, Toryn reached for Slaney's hands and then bowed his head to pray for her. He was deeply concerned with what he had been reading. There was a connection between them that he had not been aware of and that connection did not involve their university days.

"Slaney? I've read through what you have there. We need to talk. But first I need to pray with you." Toryn simply prayed for her and the situation that they had found themselves in.

"Toryn? What did you find?" Slaney knew that he had found something. She was just not prepared to hear what he said.

"I find that there is a connection between us that neither one of us knew about." Toryn reached for his notes. "Let me go through what I found and then we'll talk about it. I'll also need to reach out to Aidan as he's the investigator."

"I know that you do. I'm just tired of doing that. I feel like my life is out of control and I want it to stop." Slaney frowned at the papers on the table, causing Toryn to laugh.

"It's not the papers' fault, Slaney." He grinned as she glared at him. Then he sobered. "Now, we met during university. I can understand why you weren't involved in a lot. And there is not a lot about you out there."

Slaney nodded, knowing that he was speaking the truth about her life.

"I had to, Toryn. I was the only living witness as to what had happened to my family. I moved so many times over the years. I am tired of that. I want to find a town where I can set down roots and live my life."

"This is your town, Slaney. We're connected, like I said, in a way that I never expected. First, your father was a reporter?"

"He was for our local newspaper. He wrote crime articles, including looking back into the past." She looked at him, horror on her face. "Is that why?"

Toryn was nodding.

"That's what I am picking up on. I need to look back at his articles but somehow, he found out something that led to what happened. I wish I knew what."

Slaney was on her feet and returning with her laptop.

"I have copies of all Dad's articles in a file on here. I also have paper copies." She sat back down beside him, a frown on her face. "Will this work?"

"We'll take a look at them together. If they're from your town, you might know the people involved."

"I might but I was so young. I moved from there when I turned eighteen. I'm not sure that my memory will help us solve this."

"It might. As to how we're connected? The family that you lived with? She's related to Andrew's Phoebe. We'll need to talk with Andrew and Phoebe as well at some point."

Slaney nodded. This was just getting worse, she decided. She wanted it over. The only solution that she could see was to move towns. Only whoever it was would follow her and go after Toryn as well.

"I see. Then, I guess that we need to. What did you find?"

"Your father was working on an article about a local business owner when he died." Toryn passed over the paper to her that documented that. "This man? He's become prominent here in this town. He's not popular however with most people. And it concerns me as to what your father had documented about him."

Slaney took the paper and then read the information. Her heart sank. She had finished that article and submitted it a year ago. It had been very popular, James had told her, being picked up by newspapers in the area and also true crime programs on the local television station in her town. That could be why the man had moved. He was afraid to stay in his town, knowing that he would be arrested.

"When did he move here?" Slaney's voice was barely audible.

"When did he move here? About two years ago permanently. But he's been in business here for years. Why?" Toryn became very concerned about Slaney. He could feel the fear radiating from her. "Slaney?"

"I know why. God help me, I didn't know that he was still there or that he had moved here. What did I do?" Slaney was on her feet, running from Toryn and slamming her bedroom door behind her.

Torn stood and watched her run, not sure as to why this had affected her and caused her to react that way. He was determined to find out why. His phone was out as he took photos of the pages in front of him. He paused for a moment before he shook his head.

There was no way that Slaney would have written an article, he decided. Toryn's hands paused as he cleaned up from their meal. The thought that had been niggled at the back of his mind congealed. Slaney had indeed written that article. He would need to search for it.

Chapter 22

The next afternoon, Andrew turned to face Toryn. Phoebe had found Slaney, realizing once Toryn had stated who the family was that Slaney had been fostered by that amid and because of that, the two ladies did have a connection. Phoebe was still discovering her family.

"Toryn? You have concerns. It's not like you to reach out as you did this morning." Andrew sat in front of Toryn's desk, his eyes on the other man.

"I do. I found out yesterday that Slaney's father had research of a man in her town. And I also found out that someone has written that article. That man has moved to this town." Toryn planted his elbows on his desk. "I can't confirm who wrote it."

"And you suspect Slaney." Andrew's mind moved through the implications of that. "It could be why she was chased that day."

Toryn nodded. Andrew had confirmed his thoughts.

"That's what I think. I think that she is following in her father's steps in writing news articles but she has hidden behind a pseudonym. I worry for her."

"Yes, you would do that." Andrew was nodding as he thought through what Toryn was not saying. "She could well have done that."

"I know. I need to confront her but I'm not sure how to without causing her to run. If she runs, we can't protect her." Toryn was on his feet, reaching for the book that Slaney had given him. He handed it to Andrew. "I think that she wrote this. She won't confirm it with me."

Andrew took the book, his eyes on Toryn. He then looked down at the book, a frown on his face. Both he and Phoebe had read it. Phoebe's comment was that she feared for the author. He had agreed with her. To know that it might be Slaney worried him even more.

"If it's Slaney, how do we keep her safe? She's ready to run, Andrew." Toryn was reaching out as a police officer but also as a man trying to protect his lady.

"That's a good question. You don't have enough evidence I would suspect to put her into protective custody. And I doubt that she would be agreeable to that."

"She wouldn't. She'll fight us on that if we do try it." Toryn knew her well enough to know that she would run before she let them do that. "I need to speak with Aidan but I don't know how to do that without breaking her trust in me."

"She means more than just a victim to you, doesn't she?" Andrew's hand went up. He remembered only too well how he had felt with Phoebe and what they had faced. They had married the day after he had rescued her from the gang holding her and then fallen in love over the next weeks as they struggled to find out who had been behind what had happened to her. Toryn was familiar with her tale, her so-called father being his uncle.

Phoebe watched Slaney as that woman shifted restlessly in her chair. She wasn't quite sure how to reach out to her.

"Slaney? What are your thoughts?" Phoebe reached for Slaney's hand, just to let her know that she was not alone.

"Phoebe? I don't know what to think. Not any more. I used to have a rigid life. That's changing. Toryn is part of it. And I don't know what to do." Slaney blinked against her emotions.

"You're falling in love, Slaney, and don't have anyone that you feel you can speak with. Talk with me. Toryn has been a part of my life for as long as I can remember. He's in love with you, Slaney. He will wait until you are ready to hear that before he says anything." Phoebe frowned as Slaney began to laugh.

"He's already said that he loves me." Slaney continued to laugh, causing Phoebe to grin as well. "It was just as he was waking up in the hospital."

"And does he remember that?" Phoebe laughed harder as Slaney shook her head.

"I'm not sure that he does. He's been told that he did that." Slaney peeked towards the office door. "We need to talk but I'm not ready to do that. I just feel that I am so dangerous."

"All the ladies felt that way." Phoebe bit at her lip. "Slaney, can I ask you something?" Slaney nodded at Phoebe, waiting for her to continue. "You don't have to tell me. I know that your father was a reporter. Are you writing?"

Slaney sighed. This was a question that she had been expecting. She had thought that it would be Aidan that would be asking those questions.

"I am. I don't want anyone to know. It's too dangerous for anyone to know. I have kept that quiet for so many years." Slaney blinked harder against her emotions. Toryn had been correct. Her emotions were breaking through and that scared her. She was used to having tight control over them and no longer had that.

Andrew hesitated as he approached the living room, Toryn beside him. Something had happened, he decided, and saw Toryn nodding beside him. Phoebe had reached through somehow to Slaney and had that lady open up to her. Andrew sat beside Phoebe, an arm around her. Toryn sat beside Slaney, an arm around that lady. Andrew simply bowed his head and prayed for the couple. He knew that Phoebe was worried about Toryn. He was as well. It wasn't just about Toryn's private life. He worried about Toryn as he was getting ready to return to work. He would be doing that in the next couple of weeks.

"Slaney, what can we do for you?" Andrew's question took her by surprise.

"I don't know, Andrew. This isn't your town. I'm not sure what you can do."

"It's okay, Slaney. We work together as police forces. We'll talk with you about anything that may need to do for you and how we can protect you."

Andrew leaned forward, his elbows on his knees. He sensed that Toryn was watching Slaney very closely.

"Thank you, Andrew. I appreciate that. It's just so difficult. I have hidden for so many years." Slaney felt Toryn's arms tighten around her. "I just don't know how to do this."

"We'll work with you, Slaney." Toryn prayed for his lady, knowing that it would get much worse for her. And for him, he thought. He just wasn't sure that they would survive.

Chapter 23

Two weeks later, Toryn sat down at his office desk in the police building. He was allowed back to work on a part-time basis. He wasn't sure that he should be there but he needed to be. Aaron was still picking up on part of the work that was needed.

Aaron watched Toryn, seeing the strain that was present on his chief's face. He knew that it was hard for Toryn to walk back into his office while he was still healing. He was ready to bring Toryn up to date on what all had been happening while he had been off.

"Aaron? What's the most urgent item that I need to deal with?" Toryn sorted through the paperwork on his desk.

"That blue folder. I know that you dislike dealing with budget items but I've been working on it for you. Take a look at it and then we can discuss it. Then, the red folders. Those are the requests for transfers that you need to look over and sign off on. The green folders are ongoing investigations and we've included what all you would need. We've tried to make it as clear as we can.

"Then, the yellow folders? Those are the requests from the media that we felt you should be aware of. Some of the requests relate to you and Slaney. We've had our public relations officer dealing with them. She'll want to speak with you at some time over the next day or so."

"Thanks, Aaron. I always know that you have everything organized for me. You and Brenna, that is. Come find me in a couple of hours. I'll look through this pile and then we'll talk." Toryn was deep into the budget numbers even before Aaron had walked away.

Toryn rose a couple of hours later and stretched. He had managed to work through most of what had been on his desk that morning. A lot of it had just required his signature. He walked through the department, stopping to speak with each officer or employee before he headed for the break room. Toryn stopped for a moment as he reached for the coffee pot, his thoughts on Slaney. He missed his morning talk with her and decided that he would call her over the lunch hour. He was tired and ready to go home but couldn't as yet. Something was holding him at the office.

Aaron found Toryn studying the notices posted on the board in the break room. He studied him for a moment before he walked to stand beside him. He didn't speak, knowing that Toryn would ask what was going on.

"Aaron? You've found me for a reason." Toryn waited patiently for Aaron to speak.

"I did. Our PR officer has received a request for an interview with you. She just is not comfortable with the credentials that were presented." Aaron was waiting for the officer to finish her investigation of that person.

"She did? Keep me posted on that." Toryn gave a grimace. He was exhausted and knew that he needed to go home. He just wasn't ready to.

"Go home, Toryn." Aaron's hand on his shoulder turned him back towards his office. "An officer is ready to drive you there. You're not up to working a full day as yet."

Toryn nodded, reaching for his jacket and then walking to where the officer was waiting for him. He stared out at his town as he was driven home. He didn't catch the glances that the officer was shooting at his rearview mirror.

"Chief? We have a tail." The officer's words caught Toryn off guard.

"We do?" Toryn shifted to stare out of the back window. "They're just far enough away not to be able to get their plate number." He was frustrated at that.

"We have someone coming up behind them." The officer watched as he saw the emergency lights come on behind the car and then the car pulled over. "We've got them."

"Good." Toryn was silent until they reached his home. "Thank you, Tom." He walked slowly towards his home, pausing for a moment. He shook his head. Toryn knew that he needed to change out of his uniform before he went to find Slaney.

Slaney looked around an hour later as a tap came to her door. She walked towards the front door, not surprised to see Toryn waiting for her. Opening the door, she stood in the doorway, frowning at him.

Toryn's face was whiter than she had seen for a few days.

"Toryn? Aren't you working?"

Toryn grinned before he wrapped her into a hug and then moved her back inside so that he could close the door.

"I was but for only half days for now. What have you been up to?"

Slaney shrugged, not sure what to say. She had spent the morning in prayer and Bible study, setting aside any column or investigation that she had been working on. She had needed that break.

"Not much." She squinted at the clock. "Did you eat?"

"I grabbed a sandwich earlier. Have you?" Toryn didn't wait for an answer as he moved to set a new pot of coffee. "Slaney? We need to talk."

"That's all we do. Talk. And that is not getting us anywhere." Slaney was disgruntled at that.

"That's how it goes." Toryn turned to face her, leaning against the countertop. "What exactly is the issue that you want to raise?"

Slaney glared at him. He just had to do that, she thought.

"I don't know, Toryn. This is all getting to me. I want it over." Slaney refused to move towards him or walk away. She just wanted an argument. Only Toryn was not obliging her with that.

"I'm not fighting with you, Slaney. We will talk. You're not ready to." Toryn turned to pour their coffee. "Where do you want to drink this?" He waited patiently for her to sputter before he heard a soft voice stating on the back deck.

Slaney was frustrated even more. She wanted a fight with Toryn but he was just refusing to. This was his training, she decided, not realizing that it was his feelings for her that kept him from fighting with her. She slumped in her chair, her mug in her hand. Toryn sat nearby, his eyes on the sky. He would wait for her to speak, to spill out what she was feeling. He just didn't know how long that would take. All he could do for his lady was surround her with his prayers. He just wanted to surround her with his arms and make it all better for her.

Chapter 24

Another two weeks had passed. Toryn was back to work full time even though he wanted to be with Slaney. That lady kept sending Toryn home, a twinkle in her eye at his reluctance. He was frustrated that the investigation wasn't going anywhere. There was just no further evidence to prove or disprove what had happened.

Aidan had had to set that investigation aside and take up others. He would read through his notes every day, praying for some clue that would advance that case. There just wasn't one. He and Lyle had taken time to go back through all the notes, reports, and evidence. They had both shaken their heads.

Emma had been around, just praying with Slaney. She had not found much more information than Aidan and that was unusual. She was still digging as she could and had pulled Jace in her office into the investigation and research. They all knew that something was about to break loose and that would threaten both Toryn and Slaney.

Slaney sat back one day, her eyes on her computer. She was at a loss, she decided, and then shoved away from her desk. She reached for the small backpack that she was using for a purse and then for her car keys. Needing to get out and about, Slaney headed for the downtown area and Ben's diner. She waved at him as she found a seat, knowing from experience that she didn't have to order. Ben would bring her what she usually had.

Ben slid into a seat across from her, praying for his young friend. He knew Toryn well, having watched that man grow from a toddler to the man who he was now. He waited for Slaney to speak, knowing that she would ask what she needed to.

"Ben? What are you hearing?" Slaney knew that she was asking a question that he might not be able to answer.

"About you and Toryn?" At her nod, Ben thought through what he had heard. He had been making notes that he planned on passing on to the couple in the next couple of days. "I have some information to give you and Toryn. I'll give it to you before you leave. For now, enjoy your meal." He looked around as he heard footsteps.

Toryn stood beside the booth, surprised to find Slaney there. He slid in beside her as Ben rose and allowed Aaron to sit across from them. Slaney frowned at the two men, sure that they had tracked her down.

"I didn't know that you would be here." Toryn's smile lit up his face.

Aaron laughed at the expression on Slaney's face. He knew that Toryn was young to be a police chief, in his early thirties, but his qualifications and drive to move up the ranks had brought him to the attention of the police board. There had been no question when he applied for the vacant post. Aaron had not been interested in moving any higher. He and Toryn worked together well as a team and he knew that

Toryn cared deeply about the men and ladies who were under him.

"Yeah, well. I needed to get out." Slaney bit into her hamburger, enjoying the taste of the food.

"I know that you do. You spend a lot of time in the house." Toryn moved his arms so that his plate of fish and chips could be set down in front of him. He frowned at Aaron who was trying to control his grin.

"Aaron? You're here? What do you have to tell me?" Slaney ignored Toryn, focused on the other man.

"What do I have to tell you? That I see a beautiful, compassionate lady sitting beside a man who cares deeply for her and who she cares for just as deeply." Aaron gave a compassionate smile at her.

Slaney blushed and refused to look at Toryn. Her eyes focused on the outside of the diner. She frowned for a moment as she saw James walking towards it. How did he find her? She reached for her phone, pulling up a text message, before she was shoving at Toryn to let her up and out of the booth. She strode rapidly from the diner, heading for James.

James stopped Slaney with his hands on her arms. He studied her closely, seeing the stress and strain that she was trying hard to hide.

"Slaney? Are you done with your meal? We need to talk." James pointed to her car. "Head off. I'll follow you."

Toryn watched as Slaney drove away, not sure what had just happened. He looked at Aaron, who shrugged. He wasn't sure what had just happened but something major had to have for James to show up.

Slaney spun to stare at James as she dropped her backpack on the kitchen table. James was here and she didn't think it would be good news for her.

"James?"

"Slaney, I had a direct threat come in to my office. It was directed at the author of your columns. Someone has been reading them and has decided that you need to stop. And that he or she plans to do that in the next while. I have reached to Aidan and he will be in touch with you."

"I see. And that means I draw back into the strict protocol that we had in place. I don't like it. I don't like that. I have freedom at last and I like that."

"I know that you do. I have spoken with Don and he is reaching out to two friends of his. They will come up with a plan to allow you your freedom and yet protect you as much as we can." James was sympathetic to her plight.

Slaney sighed, her eyes closing.

"And Toryn will want to move in and protect me. I can't let him. He's still recovering from his shooting."

"He's recovered, Slaney. And yes, he will want to move in and protect you. That's who is he. And because he is interested in you, he will not walk away from you." James paced, worry uppermost in his mind. "I can't be here for you. We need to find you a lawyer here that you can work with."

Slaney snorted, knowing that James would do just that. She just didn't want to work with anyone else but him. They had a long history together of keeping her safe. She didn't know if she could trust anyone else to do that. She too paced away from James, hearing her phone chiming but ignoring it.

Chapter 25

Toryn walked towards Slaney that evening as she moved around the front yard of her home. He was not sure what to say to her. Slaney turned to face him, a shuttered look on her face.

"Slaney? Is everything okay?" Toryn waited for her to speak, not wanting to push her.

Slaney stared at him, thinking that he looked exhausted and in pain. She walked towards him and stopped just short of him. She didn't want to get too close to him for some reason. Slaney shrugged, not sure what to say.

"I don't know, Toryn. James just let me know today that someone somehow has tracked me to his office. He won't say anything but it worries us that someone has done that. We've taken as many steps as we can to try and protect us. Or at least they have tracked the name that I write under."

"How did they manage to do that? Your name isn't out there." Toryn reached to wrap an arm around her and turn her back towards the house. He seated her in one of the wicker rocking chairs and then sat himself, his eyes worried but shuttered as well. Toryn was trying to think through how that had happened.

"James is very careful about protecting who I am. No one is to know that I write those articles." Slaney didn't realize that she had just confided in him something that she had wanted to keep hidden. He would not break her trust.

"What do we do then, Slaney? If someone has found James, then they are really digging into finding you. And we need to protect you." Toryn prayed for his lady, begging God for His protection of Toryn's lady.

"I don't know, Toryn. I have trusted James all my life but I wonder now if I should." Slaney was desperate to survive and still hide from whoever it was who had murdered her family

"I know that Emma has been looking into everyone that she can in your past. If she had found something concerning, she would have reached out to you and to us. That's what she does."

"I know. She's been keeping in touch with me. She shouldn't. Emma has a family that she needs to take care of." Slaney glared at Toryn as he grinned. "This is not funny, Toryn."

"No, it's not. But your reaction is just so you. Emma considers you a friend. She looks out for her friends." Toryn rose, a hand extended to her. "Come on, Slaney. Find your purse. I'm taking you out for a meal."

Slaney stared up at him, shaking her head.

"Not tonight. You're exhausted and in pain. Go home, Toryn." She walked past him and shut and locked the front door.

Toryn stared at the door, not believing that she had just done that. He hesitated before he turned and walked slowly back to his own home. He turned as he reached the back deck, to stare towards the house that held the lady he loved. Toryn turned again and walked into his house, to his living room where he collapsed on the couch. He had overdone it that day, he realized, as he drifted off to sleep, still trying to determine what to do to protect his lady.

Sitting upright in her bed, Slaney stared around, her eyes catching the time. It was just after midnight. She shoved aside the blankets that had covered her and was on her feet, searching through her house. Slaney could not find the source of the sound that had awakened her. She sighed. There was someone outside but by the time someone came, they would be gone. Slaney leaned against the front door, listening to the sounds outside. She would look around in the morning.

Early morning found Slaney outside of her home, staring around before she began searching through the gardens. She stepped back as she found the motion-activated cameras. How had someone found her? No one should know where she was living. No one should know what town that she was in. Was this related to her or to Toryn? Slaney turned to watch Toryn's house, knowing that he would not be up yet. It was just too early.

Slaney walked back into her house, found her phone, and sent a text to Aidan. He would be around that morning as soon as he would be able to. She was tired of hiding and of living life on the run, so to say. She had tasted freedom from that with Toryn and his friends and wanted that for herself. Slaney was petitioning God for that. She knew that He was in control and was protecting her. She prayed for healing for Toryn. A thought stopped her and she prayed for healing and release for herself. Slaney had never had a chance to really grieve for her family and didn't think that she would until the person or persons responsible were apprehended.

Toryn watched as Aidan moved around the house next door. He had been heading for his truck to head for the department when he paused. He approached Aidan as he stepped back onto the driveway.

"Aidan?" Toryn sensed that Slaney was standing nearby and turned, reaching for her hand. For once, he was not the police chief but a man who wanted to take care of his lady.

"Slaney found cameras around the house this morning. We can't pick up anything from the security feed. They kept themselves well hidden." Aidan was frustrated. This was just another piece of evidence that would go nowhere. And he needed it to go somewhere if he was to solve this.

Toryn sighed to himself. He had been expecting something like this. He just wished that it had not happened. He had to head off but he asked Aidan to find him when he could. Slaney watched him walk away, feeling as if her lifeline to reality had just left.

"Slaney? What else can you tell me?" Aidan drew her attention back to him.

Slaney shrugged. Her mouth opened and shut before she made a decision.

"Aidan? You've spoken with James. I've trusted him with my life for years."

"And now you're wondering if he's involved." Aidan had come to the same conclusion. "I'm looking into him. So far, he's clean but I do have some digging to do. Don't worry. I'll keep you in the loop about what I find."

Slaney stood that afternoon, stretching before she walked back through the house. She was bored, she decided, but not sure what she wanted to do. She paused as she stepped out onto the front porch.

"Emma? You're here?" Slaney reached to hug her. "I wasn't expecting you."

"It's okay. I had to head this way anyway so I took a chance that I would find you at home." Emma grinned at her as she took her son's hand. "This is Isaac. I hope that you don't mind that I brought him."

"Not at all." Slaney reached for Isaac as he in turn had reached for her. "It's been a while since I've been around a toddler. Come on in." Slaney laughed as Isaac hugged her. "He is so sweet."

"He is for the most part. We have our struggles at times. That comes from having two strong-willed parents." Emma set down the papers that she had been holding. "Just how are you, Slaney?"

"I'm not sure, Emma. Not any more. I have so many questions. I have also tasted freedom and don't want to lose it. Can you understand that?" Slaney blinked against the surge of emotions that surprised her at how strong they were.

Chapter 26

Aidan sat back in his chair, reading through the information that he had just retrieved from his printer. He wasn't sure what he was reading but he didn't like it. He also was not ready to go to Toryn yet. On his feet, Aidan searched for Lyle, tracking him down in a small conference room. Lyle looked around as he heard footsteps, a frown on his face at the look on Aidan's face.

"I don't like that face, Aidan. What did you find?" Lyle reached for the paperwork, scanning through it. "You've verified this?"

"I am trying to but there are roadblocks all over the place." Aidan pulled out a chair and sat. "I don't get how this was missed or why I can't verify it."

"I would suspect that someone is putting this out there. Go to her hometown and talk with him. Talk with the couple who were foster parents to her. Find her parents' friends and speak with them. I'll clear you to go." Lyle watched the younger detective closely. Aidan was young to have made the detective squad but he was careful and thorough in his investigations.

"That's what I am thinking, Lyle. I'll head out this afternoon. I want this over. We're not getting anywhere with either the robbery or the shooting." Aidan rubbed at his temple where a headache was developing.

"Take George with you. That way, he can verify what you find and no one can say that you're changing any information just because you're friends with Toryn and Slaney."

Aidan nodded, having come to that conclusion himself. He was on his feet, hunting for George and then heading out to pack a bag before he swung by George's to pick that man up for the trip north. He was not looking forward to prying into Slaney's past and possibly letting someone know where she was. He had to decide how to approach it without doing that. And Aidan was not sure that he could do that.

Toryn looked up as Lyle tapped at his door and then entered his office and closed the door behind him. He frowned. Lyle only did that when he needed to speak in private with him.

"Lyle?"

"Aidan's heading for Slaney's hometown. He found information on her lawyer that he can't verify and feels that he needs to head that way to do so." Lyle was troubled by that. "I pray that he can find out some information. I'm just not sure that this will work."

"We'll pray that it does. Slaney is getting ready to run again to another town. If she does, we can't protect her." Toryn was worried about that but had had to take his worries to God.

"We will. How are you feeling?" Lyle obsessed Toryn carefully, seeing the strain that he was trying hard to hide.

"I'm getting there. It's a struggle some days but I've been in counselling with Gideon. He's giving good advice." Gideon was their pastor and a good friend to them.

"That's what you need." Lyle looked down for a moment. "How about you and Slaney coming for a meal this week? It might help her to get out of the house. I know that she doesn't do that much."

Toryn nodded. He would ask Slaney that night and then make plans based on her decision. He would not force her to do so but he had seen the openness with how she was reacting to his friends. Toryn liked the lady who was emerging. He was just afraid that she would walk away on him. He didn't know that Slaney was waiting for him to speak about his love for her.

Toryn's attention went back to his paperwork. He felt overwhelmed that day and he knew why. He was exhausted and still feeling pain at times. At last, Toryn rose and headed around the building, stopping to speak with each person present. He stood for a moment watching as prisoners were processed in the booking area, not sure who he was watching for. But he knew that he was watching for someone.

Slaney was restless as well. She stared at the laptop, for once not wanting to write. She felt overwhelmed by all that she was going through and just prayed that it would be over soon. Slaney didn't expect that to happen. On her feet, she walked away from the office and to the bedroom where she threw herself facedown on her bed. She was asleep almost instantly.

Toryn paced his office. It was almost time for him to leave but he was reluctant to. Someone was waiting for him, he sensed, and that person didn't mean him well. He turned to find a patrol officer at his door.

"When you're ready to leave, Chief, we have an escort for you. Aaron has asked that we drive you back and forth from now on." The officer waited patiently for Toryn to gather what he needed and then headed for the parking lot.

Toryn pulled into his driveway, a patrol car behind him. That officer walked the perimeter of his house before waiting for Toryn to unlock his door and then walked through his house. He nodded as he walked away, this time to walk around Slaney's home.

Watching as the officer drove away, Toryn was puzzled. Something had triggered that and he wanted to know why. His phone was out as he called Aaron.

"Aaron? Talk to me. Tell me what's going on. I don't get an escort home or be told that I'm being driven to work without something happening." Toryn dropped his keys on his kitchen counter before he turned to lean back against it.

"We had word from the street that a contract is out on you. We're working feverishly to confirm that and determine who is behind it. That came in just before you were to leave." Aaron stood in his office, staring out of his window. It was frustrating that this had happened.

"I see. And it came from a reputable source, I gather." Toryn rubbed at his temple. Somehow, he had expected this but had prayed that it wouldn't.

"It has, Toryn. One of our undercover officers got word to us. We need to find out who it was. And you know that can take time."

"Keep me updated, Aaron. Does this include Slaney?" Toryn didn't really that he was holding his breath until he heard Aaron reply in the negative. "Okay, then. I'll see you in the morning."

Slaney tapped at Toryn's door a while later, not sure if he was around. She had heard his truck pull in and then another car pull in and leave. She shivered in fear, scared that he had disappeared and would be lost to them forever.

Don approached her, not sure if she had heard him. He saw her jump as his footsteps sounded on the floor near her.

"Slaney? Are you okay?" Don had not spoken to her in a number of days and didn't think that Daci had been in contact either. Aaron had had reached out to Don to see what he could do to help.

Slaney shrugged, her eyes on Toryn as he stood in the doorway. He was fine, she realized and that made her happy. Don's eyes connected with Toryn, who nodded. Don sighed. This was why he was here, then. God had spoken to Aaron who in turn had spoken with Don.

Chapter 27

A week had passed since Aidan had headed to Slaney's hometown. He had not found the people very forthcoming with him and that surprised him. Her foster parents had been reluctant to talk, given that the murderer was still out there. They were concerned for their own family. James had been surprised to see Aidan and bluntly told him that he was placing Slaney at greater risk by coming there. Aidan was frustrated. He felt as if it had been a waste of time for him to go there. George had felt the same. Both detectives had looked at one another before George shrugged. They were really no further ahead in their investigation.

Toryn had not been surprised when Lyle spoke with him about Aidan's trip to Slaney's town and how they had not been able to find out much information regarding the murders of Slaney's family. That town was protecting her and until and unless something came up that would persuade someone there to come forward, they would not receive any information or help from them.

Slaney had looked at Aidan when he told her that he had been in her town. She frowned at that, wondering just what he had been looking for. It had not surprised her either that no one had offered any help.

"You're an outsider, Aidan. They won't talk to you. It's a small town but very close." Slaney had a thoughtful look on her face. "Just what were you trying to find out?"

Aidan nodded. They had talked many times but Aidan still felt that there was something that she was not telling him. And that one fact might be what was needed to find the villains and bring them to justice.

"I needed to talk with your police force, with your foster parents, with whoever would speak with me. It's what we do when we're investigating someone, Slaney. And you are no different than them. You are a mystery to us. We do need to find out what you know and how that might impact our investigation." Aidan waited for her to speak, not finding that she was willing to. "You need to talk with us, Slaney. Toryn's life and yours as well are at stake. I don't want to bury either one of you. Whoever this is has proven that they are not afraid to kill."

Slaney stared at him, knowing that he was correct. It was just that she had hidden for so long that fear of discovery kept her quiet. There had been many years that had passed. With each passing year, she had tucked everything deeper and deeper. Toryn was working on pulling that out of her despite her fear for him.

"I see. Aidan, do you know how hard this is?" Slaney's emotions were raw that day. It was her parent wedding anniversary and she really didn't need Aidan poking and prodding her.

"I know that it is, Slaney. I really do know that. Talk to me. At some point, you will. We are trying to find the ones responsible. We also think that Toryn was a target and you were used to get to him. Someone knows who you are and how you know Toryn. We haven't found that person yet and we need to. It might just be a simple word that brings them to justice. A name. A place." Aidan was pushing hard, feeling that he needed to.

Slaney nodded, her eyes on the floor. She wasn't ready to do that but she had to at some point. She wanted James to be there but he was away on a planned family vacation and she would not disturb him. Daci came to mind and she knew without asking that Daci would be there for her.

"I need someone with me, Aidan. Is Daci okay to do that?" Her voice wavered as she asked that.

"It would. Daci has done that before." Aidan walked away, his phone out to call Daci. "Daci? Are you at work?"

"Not at the moment. I've been working from home today. Where do you need me?" Daci locked away what she had been working on, reaching for her purse and keys. This was not the first time that an officer had called her to sit with a victim while they were giving a statement. She never refused, knowing that sometimes just a friendly face was all that was needed.

"Slaney has asked for you to come and sit with her. She's ready to talk." Aidan turned to watch Slaney, who stood in her living room, an almost crumpled look to her. He prayed for his friend, knowing that when she spoke, it would destroy what safety and protection she had built around her over the past decades. And it was decades. She was in her early thirties, he knew, and the murders had happened when she was young.

"I'm on my way. Where?"

"Her home. That's her safety net right now. She wanted James to be here but he's away on vacation."

"And we need to keep Toryn away from her while you speak with her." Daci pulled into Slaney's driveway and walked rapidly away from her car.

"That's not a problem. He's in a police services meeting, albeit reluctantly." Aidan smiled briefly as he remembered the look on Toryn's face.

"He's having second thoughts, Aidan, about working with the force. If Slaney takes off and runs, he'll be right behind her. His sole focus is not the force and his people."

"No, it's not any more." Aidan pocketed his phone, watching as Daci walked into the house. He pointed to the living room where Daci would find Slaney.

Daci hesitated for a moment in the doorway before she was across the room to hug Slaney. She then stood back for a moment before she prayed for her friend.

"Slaney? You're ready to do this?" Daci didn't think that she was but it was not her life that was at stake.

"No, I'm not but I need to. I just don't know if I can handle what happens afterwards." She didn't see Gideon, their pastor, entering as well. Aidan had reached out to him and Gideon had just left his office and came to find Slaney. It was what he did for his people and for any stranger who needed his care.

Slaney stared at Gideon before she nodded. He needed to be here too, she decided. She just had to finish before Toryn showed up. And he would show up at some point. It had become customary for them to spend the evening outside when they could or on one of their porches. On occasion, they did go out for a meal but that was a rarity.

Chapter 28

Slaney finally sat, her knees bouncing as her feet moved restlessly. She was not ready for this, she decided, and was ready to jump to her feet and run. Daci's arm was around Slaney, holding her in place. Slaney nodded as Daci moved her arm but continued to sit near her.

Gideon had simply bowed his head and prayed for Slaney, asking for peace in what she was about to say and that she would be able to articulate how she needed to. He knew from briefly speaking with her that she had hidden a lot down deep inside her. He had seen it before. Unfortunately, once they began to talk, their emotions were all over the place. Slaney had friends to help her but she needed that one person who would be there for her in the middle of the night when terror struck.

"Okay, Slaney. Just begin talking." Aidan gave her an encouraging smile and received a wavering one in return. "I'm ready when you are. And nothing you say goes beyond this room. I'll work with what you give me to find out who is responsible for what you've gone through. Daci and Gideon keep confidences. It's part of who they are and what they do."

Slaney searched the faces of the three with her. She desperately wanted Toryn to be there, to have his arm around her and for him to be holding her hand. She just knew that he couldn't be. It wasn't how it worked.

"I don't know where to start, Aidan. How do I know that?" Slaney was delaying going back in her memory. She knew that it would hurt and hurt her deeply to do so. She had grieved for her family as a youth but this was different. This time, she would be ripping open a wound that had not healed and dealing with it as an adult. She prayed for strength to do that. Her phone vibrated for a moment and she reached for it. A soft smile crossed her face as she read Toryn's text message. He was praying for her and loved her. Slaney had not heard him admit to that since he had been in the hospital. That would help get her through the next few hours.

"Okay, Aidan." Slaney turned her attention to the detective. He waited patiently for her to speak, knowing that sometimes it took victims time to speak. And Slaney was a victim in many ways. "Where do I start?"

"Tell me about your parents and brother." Aidan gave her an encouraging smile. "What do you remember about them?"

Slaney sniffed, wiping at the tears that sparkled on her cheeks. She didn't mean to weep but her emotions would let her do nothing else.

"So, I was the older of the two of us. Shannon was younger. We were close to one another. Dad was a newspaper reporter and Mom stayed at home. She wrote a home and gardening column for a local newsletter and enjoyed that. She had large beautiful gardens. Dad was so proud of her.

"Dad wrote crime columns and did reporting for the local newspaper. Some of his crime columns were picked up by local newspapers. He didn't worry too much about that. He worried that we would face danger because of it. We kept close to home but were free to go out with our friends and do things. Mom and Dad just asked that we keep in touch with them and let them know where we were. Both Shannon and I knew the reason why. We didn't want to worry anyone.

"A couple of months before what happened? Dad was beginning to worry more and more. He watched us closer than he had. I never knew why. I just knew that they were more and more concerned about where we were.

"That night? I had been asleep when I heard a noise that woke me up. I think that I heard Dad yelling and Mom screaming. There were popping sounds. I just scrambled off my bed and slid under it to hide. I covered my head with my arms and prayed that they were okay. An officer searching the house found me and carried me out of the house. I didn't know that Mom, Dad, and Shannon were all dead at that point. They shielded me from seeing anything. I never went back into that house." She paused to sip at the bottle of water that Gideon had handed her.

"They told me the next morning that Mom, Dad, and Shannon were dead and how. They questioned me on what I knew. I couldn't tell them anything. We had been protected by Mom and Dad. We have no family left. That meant I had to go into foster care. The couple that took me in was in the police services. That was the deciding factor in where I ended up.

"I have no idea who or why. James has worked with me for years to protect my identity. We took steps that shielded who I was just in case the murderers found me. We know that they are looking for me. That has been obvious over the years. James recently had a letter come to him that threatened the writer of a crime column." Slaney paused her words, needing time to compose herself. She wasn't sure that she wanted to admit to being someone who was hiding.

Aidan looked up from his notes, waiting patiently for her to continue. He suspected what she might say but he needed her to admit to him who she was. Daci frowned at Aidan and then Gideon. She had no idea what was coming.

"Aidan? What I am about to say has to stay quiet. I can't continue with my work if it comes out. I continued Dad's crime columns, using a pseudonym. I won't tell you what that name is. The column has spread in popularity over the years without my trying too hard. I have helped to bring people to justice. That's what my purpose has been. But if it means that someone close to me is threatened, I will shut it down. The pain that I went through is too great for me to want anyone else to go through it. I have also written a book based on a murder, again under another name."

"We understand, Slaney. We really do. And you have found a place to feel at home here in Oak City. You don't want to run but you will if you feel that you need to." Aidan looked down at his notes. He knew the name that she was writing under. He had read that column for years without realizing that story behind it. "I know your column, Slaney. I will not give you away but I know that I need to investigate your history further. And I will be circumspect in doing that."

"Thank you, Aidan. I appreciate that. I understand that at some point, it will come out. When that happens, they will find me."

"They already have, Slaney. They have been tracking you through the years and to every town that you go to. For some reason, they have not moved in on you. But you are on borrowed time, you do know that? James will be placed in protective custody when he returns. They have connected the column to him somehow."

"I know. I wish that this was all over." Slaney buried her face in her hands. "I just want my Mom and Dad and Shannon. I need them." She began to weep, her emotions too strong for her to control.

Daci's arms were around her friend as she tried to console and comfort her. Gideon was on his feet, heading for the outdoors. Slaney needed a parent and Toryn's parents were there. She knew them and Toria would be the one to bring comfort to her son's lady. Their friends had watched how Toryn was reacting to Slaney and knew that he had made his choice. Slaney was more difficult to read, given her history and how she had been forced to hide over the years. Toria had answered Gideon's call, simply stating that she and Tavin would be there as soon as possible.

Chapter 29

Slaney jumped as she heard more voices in her home and then felt Toria's arms come around her. The mother's prayer that was whispered in her ears had her turning to hug Toria. Slaney had come home at last, her emotional rollercoaster ride that day enough to drive her to that realization. She just wondered where Toryn was.

Sleeping at last, Slaney didn't hear the conversation around her. Gideon had left after praying for his friends. Daci stayed, knowing that at some point, Slaney would want to talk and she wanted to be there for her. Aidan had left as well, heading for the office and his investigations that were waiting for him. He was disturbed by what he had heard. Slaney had been so young when she went through the murders of her family and then had basically had to live a hidden life. That had not been what any young girl should have faced. Now, he had to track back through the newspaper columns and determine which one was the trigger to the murders.

Toryn paused as he walked towards his home that night. His parents were with Slaney? That puzzled him. He rushed to change from his uniform, locking away his service weapon, and then changing into jeans and a sweatshirt. He wanted to be with Slaney. His instincts were telling him that something had happened that day and whatever it was affected his lady.

Tavin's hand on Toryn's arm stopped his son from leaving his back porch. Tavin needed to talk with Toryn before he headed for his lady.

"Dad? What happened? I thought that you and Mom had planned to go away for the day." Toryn's gaze shot between his father and the house next door. He could hear the soft sounds of late-afternoon nature in his ears and smell the scent of a freshly mown lawn. He realized that it was his. His father had done the yard work that he had planned to do that evening.

"Slaney spoke with Aidan today. She opened up to him, from what Aidan said, about the murders and what her father did for a living in more detail. She also shared something with him that I am not sure that you are aware of."

"That she writes crime columns? I guessed that much. This makes no sense though. How did they find her?" Toryn was struggling to understand the fact that Slaney had finally spoken with Aidan. He had guessed that fact and she had confirmed it, simply asking that he not tell anyone until she had to. Apparently, that time had come today.

Tavin nodded, knowing that his son and his lady were talking. He had suspected as much.

"Let's get you to your lady, son. She's slept a lot today."

"She would." Toryn still hesitated to walk down the steps. "Her emotions are all over the place." He still didn't move. "Thanks for doing the lawns, Dad."

"That's not a problem, son. You're still struggling with your healing even though you're back at work and mostly healed. It's what you would do for me." Tavin's arm was across his son's shoulders, wondering that the little newborn he had first held all those years ago was now a man grown and well respected in their town. "Let me pray for you. God has you in His hands and is moving this along at His pace. He is protecting and defending you."

"I know that, Dad. It's just sometimes hard to accept that we're not in control." Toryn walked away from his house, Tavin keeping pace with him. He found Slaney on the back patio, watching him. She simply moved into his open arms, finding comfort from his touch. Tavin lightly laid a hand on Toryn's shoulder and then Slaney's head before he walked past them, a heaviness in his heart. This adventure was far from over.

"Okay, sweetheart?" Toryn's voice was low as he just held the love of his life.

Slaney shrugged, not sure what to say. She looked up at him, seeing his emotions in his eyes. She tightened her hug on him before stepping back.

"I'm not sure, Toryn. I am really not sure. Aidan did need to know. I don't know that if I had told him any earlier if it would have mattered. I don't know that what happened here is related to what I went through." Slaney paced, her emotions not letting her stay still.

"That's what he'll work through. I imagine that he has had suspicions and that is why he headed to your hometown. This has increased your danger." Toryn was more than a little worried about her.

"I know. It also increases yours. They've connected us somehow." Toryn was still puzzling that one through without any concrete answers.

"I don't see how. We only were acquaintances at university. I hung around the edge of your group just because someone asked me to." She paled, a thought crossing her mind. "Toryn? Why was I asked to join your group of friends?"

Toryn paused as his hand rubbed at the back of his neck. He hadn't realized that was why Slaney was there. He didn't know that someone had asked her to join.

"Slaney? Who asked you?" His hand reached to turn her back into the house, his parents surprised at their sudden appearance as Toryn almost ran her into the building.

"Jeff Watson. Wasn't he a friend of yours?" Slaney turned to face him.

"Not really. He wasn't a part of our group. That is odd, you know." Toryn's phone was out as he sent off a text message to Aidan and then one to Emma. Emma, he knew, would be in touch as soon as she could.

"I never knew that. I thought that he was a friend of yours." Slaney stared at Toryn in horror. "What did I do?"

"You didn't do anything, Slaney." Toryn turned as he heard his father speak. "What was that, Dad?"

"Where was this Watson from?" Toryn's question had the couple looking at each other.

"Watson? He was from north of us." Toryn looked at Slaney. "Slaney?"

"He's from my town. I didn't recognize him as he is two or three years older than me. That's our connection. Him." Slaney looked horrified at the thought.

Toryn was reaching for his phone, sending off a text message to Aidan. Aidan responded that he had the name and was investigating the man. He had not expected Slaney to make the connection. And that made it even worse for Slaney. If he had asked her to join a group that she was not part of but Toryn was, what else had this man plotted?

Chapter 30

Toria absolutely refused to leave Slaney. She was afraid for the young lady who had become like a daughter to Tavin and herself. She had sent Tavin back to their home to retrieve what they needed to stay with Slaney. Toryn had stared at his mother, knowing her heart and then just giving her a hug with a thank you whispered in her ear.

Slaney had stared at Toria and then hugged her before walking away, Toryn following her. His hand stopped her forward walk.

"Slaney? Talk to me." Toryn refused to let her walk any further away from him.

"What can I say, Toryn?" She stared up at him with a shuttered look on her face. "I brought this trouble to you."

"We don't know that, Slaney. I could have brought it to you." Toryn stared down at her. "A question, Slaney. How many people knew that your father wrote those columns?"

Slaney stared back at him, not sure why he was asking what he was.

"I don't know, Toryn. As far as I know, no one did. He did the true crime columns under a different name. The only one who knew was James." Her face paled. "Is he the one behind this?" Slaney jumped as she heard Aidan's voice behind her. "Aidan?"

"It's not James." Aidan's voice was stern as was his face. Toryn frowned at him, knowing that something had happened.

"What happened to James?" Toryn's quiet voice and question brought Slaney's eyes to his face before she spun back to face Aidan.

"Someone got to his house, Toryn. It was burnt down last night. James was not home. We have put him into hiding along with his family." Aidan didn't move his eyes from watching Slaney. "If you need to contact him, do that through me. He's very worried about you, Slaney."

"He's safe?" At Aidan's nod, her eyes slid closed as she struggled with her emotions. "I was worried about him. I won't call or text or email him unless I go through you." Slaney felt Toryn's arms around her and she leaned back against him.

"Do that, Slaney. It may be the only way that you stay alive. Whoever it is that is after either you or Toryn has shown that they do not care if someone dies. Toryn? We have linked the robbery to the attempt on your life. Someone has come forward with that detail. Slaney was recognized and they were following her for a number of days. They were aware that you were in the same friends' group at university. The robbery was staged in the hopes that you showed up. You didn't so they had to take other steps. They saw both you and Slaney that morning. These men meant business. And now we don't know who is out there watching you."

Slaney walked away, shoving Toryn's arms from around her. She didn't want to hear that someone else was out there. She was watching around herself but still felt threatened. *God, please protect Toryn and his parents and his friends.* This was her hourly prayer. She had memorized all the verses about fear, hope, peace, protection, and defense that she could. She just didn't know how God would protect her.

Toryn watched her walk away, a frown on his stern face. He knew Aidan was not saying something. He jerked his head towards the back door, stalking that way and hearing Aidan's footsteps following him.

"What did you not say, Aidan? I know you too well. You have more news that you can't share with Slaney." Toryn spun to face the detective, a haunted look momentarily on his face.

"There is, Toryn. You and I have done this job for far too many years not to know what happens. There is a contract out on you. We can't determine who or why as yet but our sources on the streets are working this as hard as they can. Word is trickling in on that but we don't have enough information to determine that. Slaney is also at risk. Just why that is, we don't know either." Aidan didn't hear Slaney moving up behind him.

Toryn watched Slaney as she hesitated and then stopped walking as she heard what Aidan had to say. His prayers were for his lady. He couldn't be with her all the time as much as he wanted to be.

"What steps do we take next, Aidan? I know what I would recommend but I am staying hands off. After all, I am a victim of crime even though I am a police officer. You'll arrange escorts back and forth for me. It's Slaney that we need to be concerned about. She's out and about without anyone with her most times. It would not take much for her to disappear." Toryn continued to watch Slaney over Aidan's shoulder. Slaney had a brief look of fear on her face before it turned to determination. He also watched as she spun on her heel and disappeared.

The soft closing of the door behind him alerted Aidan to the fact that someone had been there. He frowned at Toryn who nodded.

"She heard?" Aidan had not wanted that to happen.

"Some of it. Not all. But she will ask me, that much I know." Toryn walked past Aidan. "Do what you need to do, Aidan. I'll talk to Don or Richard and see what we can do about bringing in someone to help protect her. And we'll have a fight on our hands."

Aidan nodded, having already reached out to Don and Richard. Those two men were willing to help as they could and planned on meeting with Aidan and Aaron in the morning. Abe Finlay had also reached out, ready to be there for Toryn and Slaney as well.

Slaney was waiting just inside the door for Toryn. With a hand on his arm, she drew him away from that room and to her office. Toria was preparing a meal and Slaney didn't want her to hear her questions.

"Toryn? What was that all about?" Slaney folded her arms across her abdomen and waited for him to speak.

Toryn sighed. He didn't know how much that she had heard of his conversation with Aidan.

"What did you hear?" Toryn waited patiently for Slaney to speak.

"Everything you two said." Slaney was deeply afraid for Toryn but not herself.

"You did? Then, you know what we know. We have security teams that will move in if we need them."

"And you think that we will?" Slaney was praying that this would not happen. She didn't realize just how deep the danger was.

"I do, Slaney. I'll have a driver back and forth to work. You won't have anyone with you. And we need to do that. If they can get to you, they'll get to me. The same for Mom and Dad. We need to watch out for them." Toryn reached to hug her, holding on to his lady just a little bit tighter and longer.

Chapter 31

Two days later, Slaney paused as she walked into a store in the downtown area of Oak City. She turned for a moment, a frown on her face. She was being followed. Her phone was out as she took a photo of the woman who was pretending not to be following her.

Jumping as a voice spoke beside her, Slaney stared at Thomas. Don had been around the day before and just told her that when she was out and about, one or more of his team would be there, running interference for her. She was not impressed with this. Slaney had come to value and appreciate the freedom that she had finally found and didn't want to lose it.

"Thomas? Where did you come from?"

"I followed you from your home, Slaney." He nodded towards the woman. "Is she following you?"

"I think so. I took her picture but I'm not sure who to send it to." Slaney bit at her lip.

"Send it to Aidan and to me. He'll try and find out who she is. So we will. My team is working on this as well, Slaney. We want to meet with you and Toryn this Saturday, if you have the time." Thomas grinned as she frowned at him.

"Okay." Slaney wasn't sure about all this. It was new territory for her and she needed Toryn there to walk through it with her. Her knight in shining armour was becoming more and more important to her.

"That's all right, Slaney. Even though we are involved in security, we were all scared for our ladies and ourselves. It's not easy to trust God in situations like this. That's what faith is. We believe in something that we can't see and that is hard to do when you really need a human to hold on to. Talk to any of us, Slaney. I know that Taran and the other ladies want to meet with you for Bible study and prayer and as a support for you. Is it okay if Taran calls you?"

Slaney nodded. This was not something that she had ever had. Her life had been too restricted and sheltered for too many years. Now, she could feel the end coming to this whatever it was that you wanted to call it. And she was off on an adventure with Toryn that didn't seem to have an ending in sight. She was so worried about him.

Toryn turned from the whiteboards in the conference room at Don's office building that Satuarday morning. Slaney's hand was tight in his. She was scared and for once had told him that. He had hugged her and kissed her temple, praying for her as he did so. Toryn had not been aware that Don's team had found so much information. He heard other voices and felt a hand on his arm. Turning, he greeted Andrew and Phoebe. Richard's team and their spouses were there. And so was Bill and Cora. He was not surprised to see Emma and Abe and his team and their wives. It was planned to spend the day working on this and then have a barbecue for their evening meal just to relax and try and get the couple's minds off what they were facing.

Slaney was in a standoff with Emma. She was shaking her head. There was no way that her father would have found that information and not acted on it. He would have written a column, she maintained, that would have exposed the murderer of the town judge.

"Your father had information on that, Slaney, and was working to prove it. I have spoken with James and Aidan. They confirmed it." Emma's face held compassion for the other lady.

"Is that why? Is that why my family was killed?" Slaney has become desperate for answers, wanting to put the past behind her and move on with her life, a life that she hoped and prayed included Toryn.

Emma reached to hug her. This was coming to a climax, Emma knew, and would be over but it was also the most dangerous time for both Slaney and Toryn. She didn't know if they would survive or how bad it would exactly get for them.

Toryn had turned to watch the two ladies, listening silently to what they were saying. Abe, Don, and Richard had cornered him to discuss options to keep the two of them safe. Abe focused on Toryn and then Slaney, seeing Emma with that lady.

"Toryn? What can you tell us?" Richard spoke up.

"Not a lot, Richard. Unfortunately, not a lot. I wish I had more information for you." Toryn was frustrated at that. "You would need to talk to Aidan. In fact, that is likely a good idea."

The three men shared a look. They had in fact spent a couple of hours with Aidan the day before. He had shared only what he could and those facts worried the three. They were only too well aware of the danger that both Slaney and Toryn faced in the next few days and weeks. None of them doubted that whatever would be coming would happen over the coming days.

"We need to go over the information that we have for you, Toryn. And Slaney needs to be a part of it." Don had had long talks with Toryn over the years about protecting victims. And Toryn was now in that position being a victim of crime with a contract out on his life. "We need to put protection in place for both you and Slaney. How do we do that?"

Toryn nodded, knowing that Don was correct. He was working with his officers to provide transportation back and forth to his office but that left his downtime not covered. He was well aware that anything could happen at any time.

"What do you three suggest? And I know that you have met with Aidan. It's what I would have done."

"We have, Toryn." Richard spoke up, his eyes on Slaney. He watched as she moved restlessly as she was deep in conversation with Kataleen and Emma.

"Okay, then. I guess that we have companions during our time off." Toryn was frustrated. He wanted to date Slaney but didn't want to at this point just to prevent any suggestion that he was dating a witness to his own attack.

"You do. Between the three of us, our teams will come up with a schedule to do that. Slaney will be the one who is more difficult to cover. She works from home but takes off to do research or to wander the town on her own. We can't have that. If you are the real target, she will be used to get to you, Toryn. Everyone is aware that she is becoming more than just a friend to you. God will direct us and protect you. It's just that His protection may not be what we would do. His ways are above our ways."

"That they are. I am trying to trust, guys. It's hard to do that at times. I don't want Slaney hurt or my parents hurt. But I am well aware that can happen. I don't like that thought but God is in control." Toryn was sober as he stated his feelings. He cried out daily to God for this to be over and to protect his lady and his parents. He just didn't like what he knew could happen. Toryn had seen it all too often in his work.

Chapter 32

Slaney felt herself growing more and more distraught as she listened to the conversation around her. This was not ending, she decided, and she had to come up with a way to do that. Her mind searched for a way and then she made a decision.

Murphy, Abe's partner and team member, had been watching her. He moved to sit beside her, a hand on her arm as she went to rise and walk away.

"Don't do it, Slaney." His voice was low as he spoke to her.

"Do what?" Slaney stared at him, no expression on her face but her eyes showed that she had made a decision, as hard as it had been to do that.

"Put yourself out there. Not until we have security in place for you. And that will happen as of tomorrow. Toryn is in agreement with it." Murphy was stern with his words. "He's in love with you, Slaney. As an officer, though, he is reluctant to approach you and tell you that when you are both victims. There are those who would say that you trapped him into that." His hand went up at her protest. "We know that you didn't, Slaney. It's not in your character to do that. However, he is the police chief here and needs to be very careful in how he approaches you."

"I can't go on like this, Murphy. I have to do this for far too many years." Slaney bit at her lip. "I asked Emma about James. She won't say what she found."

Murphy nodded, well aware of how Emma worked. She would not accuse anyone unless and until she had confirmation of what she suspected.

"She has doubts about him, Slaney. We've talked about this. Our team has been working through what we can as have Don and Richard's teams. That's why we're here today, to go over everything with you. Can you work with us on that?"

Slaney nodded, her eyes on Daci who had appeared. Daci had spent the evening with Slaney and the two had spent a long time in prayer. Then, Slaney had questioned Daci on who she thought was behind it all. Daci had hesitated for a moment before she began to speak.

Daci had been honest with Slaney. She questioned James' involvement in it all. After all, she stated, he was the one who knew what her father did and was the only one who knew what Slaney actually did. Slaney had stared at her friend, her face going white.

"He's involved?" Slaney's words had barely been audible.

"We think so. Thomas and Joshua have found some information on him that can't be explained. Slaney, we need you to go back over all your interactions with him, what you can remember about him and his family, and what your feelings are."

Slaney had snorted, bringing a smile to Daci's face. She had been doing that. On her feet, she was into her office and back again, handing Daci a file folder.

"This is what I have discovered, Daci. I don't see that he's involved but there may be something that I am not finding. I pray that he isn't. But it does make some sense in how he has kept me hidden."

"That is true. Aidan will have spoken with the detective in charge of that cold case. He has not said what he has found and rightly so. Now, what do we do with you? You know that Don is going to want to move his team in when he can to protect you when you're around town on your own."

"I know that he will. That doesn't mean that I have to like it, does it?" Slaney gave a small grin as Daci laughed.

Slaney's mind came back to the present. She searched Murphy's face, seeing the concern there that he felt.

"How do we do this? We can't do it forever. I've had enough of hiding and being restricted. I have had no friends until now. How do I go back to that, Murphy? I'm not ready to." Slaney's voice had risen slightly, bringing eyes to her and Murphy.

"Work with us, Slaney. Work with our three teams. We don't want to see you hurt any more than you have been. And that can happen even with our protection. We don't want that for you or for Toryn." Murphy leaned forward, his elbows planted on the table. He was assessing what they needed to do and how to do it. "For now, we work with Don and his team. When he is not able to be with you or Toryn, then either Richard's team moves in or ours does. Richard has the two ladies on his team, which makes sense for him to be here."

Slaney finally nodded. She was well aware of the danger that was stalking both herself and Toryn. She would do what she could to keep him safe, even if that meant moving to another town. Slaney had packed her things that morning, ready to climb into her car and drive away. She suspected that Toryn was well aware of how she was feeling and that he would do anything he could to prevent her from doing that, even to the point of running with her.

"What do I do then, Murphy? How do I stay safe and keep everyone around me safe?"

Murphy nodded. He knew that she was informed about what she was facing. Their plans would depend on her compliance with them. And he was not sure that she would.

"Don is planning on putting one of his men with you every day. If you do go out, then another one goes with you. It is imperative that you follow what we ask you to do. It may mean your life or the life of someone around you." Murphy slid over a sheet of paper. "These are our plans. And the three team leaders have worked together with Aidan to come up with this. Do you have any questions?"

Slaney read through the list, noting that it really wasn't much different from how she had lived her life, other than having someone with her when she was out and about. She didn't like that but understood the reasoning.

"I don't like this, Murphy, but I understand why. How long?"

"How long? That we don't know, Slaney. We will work with you every day and every step of the way. We just need you to work with us. Aidan tells me that he is working diligently to solve this and soon."

"I know that he is. So am I." She stared past Murphy at Toryn who had moved in on them. "Toryn?"

"I agree with the team leaders, Slaney. I want to keep you safe and will do the best that I can." Toryn pulled Slaney to her feet and then to the outdoors. He needed to be outside for some reason and he wanted Slaney with him.

Slaney protested at Toryn's tug on her hand. She was not ready to go with him. She wanted to stay inside and go over everything.

"Toryn? What are you doing? Let me go!" Slaney pulled away from Toryn and paced through the yard.

Toryn watched her, knowing that she was frustrated with the restrictions that would need to be placed on her. She was willing to do that, he was sure. He was just as frustrated. Toryn looked around as he heard a sound, a frown on his face, before he was racing towards Slaney. He just wasn't in time. The small shed near the back of the yard where Don stored his garden tools exploded, sending Slaney flying through the air to land in a crumpled heap, her face buried in the grass. Toryn was spun around by the blast and then too was on the ground, his head hitting hard.

Chapter 33

Struggling to a sitting position, Toryn searched for Slaney. Seeing her motionless body yards from himself, he attempted to rise, falling backwards to land on his hand again and again. He finally just gave up on rising to his feet and on hands and knees, Toryn crawled towards her, ignoring the pain that wracked his body. A hand on Slaney's back let him know that she was still alive. Shifting to a sitting position, Toryn struggled to draw her into his arms. Her head lolled against his shoulder as he cradled her to him. He knew that he was unable to rise and prayed for help. His hand brushed the hair from her face as he watched for her to rouse. Only Slaney didn't do that.

Unable to hear anything at the moment with the loud ringing in his ears, Toryn jumped as he felt a hand on his shoulder. He looked up to see Matt, the paramedic on Abe's team, reaching for Slaney. He was reluctant to give her to anyone else but surrendered her to Matt and Thomas' care. Each team had a paramedic on it. Thomas was the paramedic on Don's team. Stephen, Richard's team paramedic, knelt beside Toryn, drawing his attention from Slaney.

"Toryn?" Stephen was trying his best to get Toryn to respond. Toryn shook his head and regretted it, his eyes closing against the vertigo that hit. "Toryn? Can you hear me?" Stephen's hand tapped at Toryn's shoulder.

"No. I can't hear you. Slaney?" Pointing to his ears, Toryn tried to shove Stephen aside but was stopped as Joshua and Nathaniel, team members for Don and Abe, moved in to prevent it.

Don looked around and then headed for his shed, Abe and Richard at his side. He was too careful when he was storing his equipment. There was no way that it should or could have exploded as it did.

"Someone set it, Don." Abe walked back around the shed to stand beside his friend. "There is no way that happened on its own." He watched as the firefighters worked to control the small fire that was the shed and extinguish the small fires on the surrounding lawn.

"I know. There is gas in there but it's stored safely. There is no way that it would have exploded." Don shifted how he was standing to look back at Toryn and Slaney.

The city paramedics had taken over the care of the two. Slaney was already moved from the site towards a paramedic rig. Toryn was still protesting leaving Slaney. Joshua and Nathaniel were holding him down for the paramedic to be able to assess him. That didn't mean that Toryn was not struggling to rise. The men's hands tightened on him.

A patrol officer turned from the burnt-out shell of the shed and walked towards Toryn. He frowned when Toryn didn't respond to his questions. He turned his head as Joshua spoke.

"What was that?"

"He's having trouble hearing at the moment." Joshua looked up at the officer. "And we can't get him to stay still."

"They were that close?" The officer looked between where Toryn was seated on the ground and the shed.

"It would seem so." Joshua rose to his feet as the paramedics convinced Toryn to the stretcher and strapped him onto it. He knew that Toryn was afraid for Slaney. With her not moving at all, that heightened his worry. "They had come outside together. It wasn't too long after they came out that we heard the explosion. By the time that we arrived out here, Toryn had Slaney in his arms. I can't tell you how hard it was to see that."

"I can imagine. Toryn will want to be with her. And we'll make that happen. No one else was hurt?"

"Not physically. Emotionally? We're struggling." Nathaniel spoke at last. He frowned as he looked around. Everyone who had been inside was now outside. He walked away, heading for Elizabeth, his wife, and wrapping her into his arms.

"Nathaniel? Is Toryn all right?" Mark had stayed back, watching around the area for the assailant as had the other men.

"No, I don't know that he is. He's having trouble hearing at the moment and is disoriented." Nathaniel rubbed at his face. "He's heading off to be properly assessed. We need to have people with Slaney. I know that officers will be assigned but we need to move in as well."

The men all looked at each other before they sorted themselves out. Some of the men headed for the hospital as did their wives. Andrew and Phoebe headed for Tavin and Toria, knowing that they would need support of family even if they were no longer that.

Tavin and Toria waited for word on Toryn, worried about their son. Aaron and Aidan had both found them, trying to reassure them but feeling as if they failed in that task. The couple had stared at the patrol officer who had appeared on their doorstep with news about Toryn, their eyes rising to where Andrew and Phoebe waited. They had no words to speak as Andrew tucked them into his truck and then drove off.

The physician turned from Slaney, reaching for the chart that the nurse was holding out for him. He made his notes before he looked back at Slaney.

"Where are her next of kin?" He waited for the nurse to speak before he turned back. "Her next of kin?"

"She doesn't have any listed. I know that she is close friends with Toryn. His parents are in the waiting room. I can put them down as next of kin. I was told that she has no living family." The nurse was saddened at that, not knowing how it would feel.

"She doesn't? I know Tavin and Toria. By all means, put them down. They would be agreeable to that. Now, let's see what we need to do." The physician moved to study the X-ray and ultrasound pictures that were available. He nodded. There were no broken bones even though there should be. A lot of bruising and soft tissue injuries were what he was expecting to find and a concussion that would be natural in the explosion.

Tavin and Toria looked up at last and rose to follow the nurse back to where their son was being treated. They hesitated at his bedside, seeing the bruising that had begun to appear on his face. Toria's hand rested on her son's cheek, tears on her cheeks. She looked around, wanting to know where Slaney was.

The nurse beckoned Toria to follow her, leaving Tavin beside his son. The nurse paused outside Slaney's door, a hand resting on Toria's arm.

"We understand that Slaney doesn't have any family or next of kin."

Toria nodded, saddened at the news. They had discussed that with her and Slaney just shrugged her shoulders. She had no one who she could ask, she told them. Toria had talked her into going to their lawyers and drawing up powers of attorney with Slaney. Toryn had insisted on being part of it. He knew at some point he would want to be part of Slaney's life for however long they both lived.

"She doesn't. Toryn, Tavin, and myself are considered that. We have the paperwork if you need to see it." Toria saw the nurse nodding at her response.

"That's what we thought. We put you down as that. In you go. She's still unconscious. The physician will be in shortly to speak with you."

Toria nodded, her attention on Slaney. She walked towards the younger woman, paying no attention to the equipment that surrounded the younger lady. She laid a hand on Slaney's and prayed for her young friend.

Tavin was worried as well about their son. Toryn had not roused as his father had laid a hand on his shoulder. Tavin too prayed for his son. He had no idea what all had happened but he would find out as soon as he could.

Aidan paced the hallway, dodging the nurses and other staff who were working. He worried about his chief and his lady. He had received word from the investigator on the scene that there had been a bomb that had destroyed the shed. Don could not give any information as to what happened. He had locked the shed the afternoon before after doing his yard work and had not been near it since then. Aidan knew how careful Don would be with his equipment. This just added to what he was investigating.

Chapter 34

Toryn raised his head slightly, frowning as he gazed around. The hospital again? Toryn's head went back against the pillow, his eyes closing. He had no idea what had happened but something had to have for him to be back here. He felt a hand on his shoulder and jumped, his eyes springing open as he stared at the man standing beside him.

"Dad?" Toryn had to swallow hard to be able to speak. "What happened?"

Tavin studied his son, worry in his eyes. No one could explain who had set the bomb or how it had been triggered.

"A bomb went off in Don's garden shed. You and Slaney were injured." Tavin waited for Toryn to ask about Slaney, a frown on his own face when Toryn didn't.

Toryn struggled to understand what his father was saying but fatigue and pain drove him back to sleep. And he slept this time, shifting to his side and pulling the covers up tight on his neck. He didn't feel his father's hand on his head as he prayed for his son before he found the chair that he had claimed earlier that evening. It was almost midnight, Tavin knew, but it would be a long night. He also knew that Toria was with Slaney, refusing to leave the younger lady.

Toria crept into Toryn's room, the door held open for her by the officer who stood on duty at the door. He gave her an encouraging smile, taking in the worry that lined his chief's mother's face. The force was determined to find the men or women responsible for this latest attack on him and his lady. Whoever it was? Their time was limited.

Tavin was on his feet, reaching to hug his wife of so many years. They had worried about and prayed for their son over the years but more so in the last few weeks. They had just taken Slaney into their family, knowing how their son felt about her by how he was reacting to her. Slaney was important to Toryn and that made her important to them.

"Toryn was awake for a bit. He's sleeping now." Tavin kept his voice low, not wanting to break the silence. He could feel the presence of God in the room and felt the hush that came with that. That Toryn and Slaney would be healed? He had no doubt that God would do that.

"That's good." Toria's hand rested on her son's shoulder, her own prayers begging God for healing for their son and his lady.

"How's Slaney?" Tavin waited patiently for Toria to control her emotions.

"She was awake a while ago and talked with Aidan. She couldn't say much other than that she and Toryn had gone outside to talk and then she doesn't remember what happened. She was horrified to hear that Toryn had been hurt again because of her. That doesn't make sense to me, love. Why would she be hurt because of Toryn?"

"Because if someone is trying to get to Toryn and take him out of his position as chief, they would use the lady who is important to him. They could go after us, but to go after a lady that he is interested in made it worse. He would do just about anything to keep her safe."

"Yes, he would. I was speaking with Don earlier. He feels guilty because it was his shed. He told me that they found the trigger to the bomb. It was set off remotely. He just doesn't understand how it was placed." Toria knew that Don was puzzled by that. He could give no answers when asked about it.

"That is strange. I would suspect that someone got in when he had the shed unlocked and was cutting the grass at the front of the house. They can come in from behind his property and be in and out without really being seen." Tavin had walked that property many times with Don.

"That is what Aidan is thinking. Aidan is wearing out, Tavin. What can we do for him?"

"I have no idea, love. We'll see what we can do for the force as a whole. Bruce Carey from the Barnabas Foundation has reached out to ask what they can do."

"He has? Yes, he would do that, given what Barnabas and all the men there went through." Toria began to pace before she turned back to Tavin, welcoming his hug. "I need to get back to Slaney."

Tavin kissed his wife, walking out into the hallway with her and then down the few doors to Slaney's room. He stepped inside for a moment to watch Slaney before he headed back for his son. They were coming up to the hard part of it all, he knew, and someone or something was out there. He just had no idea who or why.

Aidan never left his office that night. He curled up on a couch in his office and caught a couple of hours of sleep before he was on his feet and heading for the crime lab. The push was on to solve this. They were all well aware that both Toryn and Slaney could have been killed the day before. That angered the force and the men and ladies of the force were determined to find the ones responsible. Aidan just wasn't sure that they would be in time. All he could do was pray for God's protection on his friends and for the answers that they needed. The answers were coming but very slowly, too slowly in his mind.

"Greg? What can you tell me?" Aidan stopped beside the tech, who had looked up at Aidan as he entered the lab.

"It's what we thought. It was set off remotely. I don't understand how the trigger survived."

"God did that, Greg. He knew that we would need that piece of evidence. We just need to find the one who built it."

"It was an expert, Aidan. I can tell you that much. And that makes me fear for the chief." Greg looked down at the pieces of whatever it was they had found. He was just not sure what all it was.

"Keep me updated, Greg." Aidan walked away towards his car. He was heading for the hospital, praying that Toryn would be awake and able to speak with him.

Tavin looked around as he heard the door open and then footsteps. Aidan was there but he would not be speaking with Toryn. Toryn was still sleeping and had been since he had been awake the evening before.

"How is he?" Aidan kept his voice low, uncertain as to whether conversation would awaken the chief.

"He was awake for a couple of minutes last night. He's been sleeping since then. The same with Slaney. Toria is with her still."

Aidan nodded, waiting for a while before he sighed and walked out of the room. Toryn had not awakened. He headed down the hallway and away from the room to find Toria pacing in the hallway outside Slaney's room. His hand on her arm stopped her.

"Toria?" His eyes were on the door.

"It's okay, Aidan. Slaney is awake but the nurse is with her. She wants to leave here and run from this town. She doesn't want anyone else hurt." Toria was distressed at that.

"We won't let her. She's in protective custody for now." Aidan watched as the nurse exited the room before his hand directed Toria back into it. He walked to the bed and then stood, watching Slaney.

Slaney stared towards the window, her fingers picking at the blanket. To hear that she and Toryn had been near a bomb that had exploded had not been what she had expected to hear. She wanted to run and run as far as she could. Only Toryn would not be with her and she refused to leave him. Slaney jumped as she heard a voice and turned to face Aidan.

"Aidan? Can I leave?" Her voice was barely audible.

"Soon, Slaney. I just need to talk with you some more." Aidan grinned for a moment at the frown that she shot his way.

Chapter 35

That Slaney was hurting more than physically was obvious. No one could look at her and doubt that she was emotionally raw and mentally spent. Her spirit was beaten down and she was having trouble trusting. She stared at the hospital room ceiling, doubting that her prayers even reached that and she decided that she just might as well give up praying. God didn't seem to be protecting them. Slaney forgot that God did indeed protect them. She and Toryn were still alive. If God had not been there, they would have perished. Slaney was extremely worried about Toryn but was refusing to ask anything about him. That was just who she was.

Daci and Jincy appeared in her room, bringing in a meal that they both hoped Slaney would eat. There were no guarantees that she would. Hugging her, they stood back, frowning at her.

"Slaney? What's going on?" Jincy spoke up, knowing somewhat how she would feel.

Slaney shrugged. She just wasn't able to put into words how she felt. She felt beaten down, she decided, and wanted to escape that. Only she had no way of knowing how to do that. She was physically ready to leave the hospital room. She just didn't want to walk away from where she knew that Toryn was. And Aidan was to come back and brief her on what he knew. How could he do that if she wasn't there?

Daci shared a look with Jincy before she pulled Slaney from her bed and shoved a bag of clothes in her hands.

———

"Go and get dressed, Slaney. We're breaking you free after we eat. You need to get out of here." Daci grinned at her. "Toryn is being released this afternoon. He'll be looking for you."

Slaney stared at them for a moment before she snapped her mouth closed. She shrugged, disappeared into the bathroom and then was back with the two ladies to enjoy their meal. She looked up as they finished, her eyes narrowed.

"You're up to something, Daci."

"I am. I have an appointment for you to have your hair trimmed and your nails done. It's my gift to you. And then I'm taking you to my place. The ladies are meeting us there. They have gifts for you." Daci gave a sad smile at the look on Slaney's face. "It's what they want to do for you, Slaney."

"I know. It's just that I have never had friends to do things with. You ladies are such a close group."

"And we have expanded to include you, Slaney." Jincy reached to hug her. "You need us and we need you."

"You do?" Slaney walked towards the door, opening it and finding Joshua and Caleb waiting for them. She frowned at their grins. "And I suppose that you are the security personnel for today?"

"We are, Slaney. Let's get you ladies to where you need to be and then we'll talk." Joshua grinned at her again. "We'll do our best, Slaney."

"I know that you will." Slaney sighed, recognizing the harsh way that she had responded.

"I'm sorry, Joshua. It's just getting to be too much. I'm not sure who to trust or where to go."

"It's understandable, Slaney. We all felt like that at some point." Joshua drove away from the hospital, a hand raised to acknowledge Aidan. "We'll do what we can."

"I know. I just don't want anyone hurt." Slaney stared out of the window. "Do we know anything, Joshua?"

"We do. We want to talk with you this afternoon after the team that's training has left. We'll meet with you at Daci's. And yes, Toryn will be there." Joshua had spoken with Toryn that morning and was very concerned about how rocky Toryn was on his feet.

Slaney studied Toryn early that evening. He was not well, she could tell, and that worried her. If he was not well, then he could not work. And it was all her fault. She had brought this to him.

Toryn wrapped an arm around her, his chin resting on the top of her head. His lady was discouraged and ready to run. He wouldn't allow that, he knew. If she ran, he would be beside her.

"Talk to me, Slaney. Tell me what you're thinking. Don't even think about running away from me. I won't let you. You're too important for me to lose track of you again." Toryn waited patiently for her to gather her thoughts and speak.

"I'm too dangerous, Toryn. Look what happened!" Slaney struggled to escape from Toryn but was unable to.

———

"We do not think that it is you, Slaney. We think it's me. That's what the evidence is showing. It's directed at you to get to me."

"I don't understand." Slaney grew quiet and still, something that she was prone to do when she became very frightened or worried.

Slaney's stillness worried Toryn. He had not seen her at this point yet and he had no idea how to reach her. He tilted his head to study her face, a frown on his own.

"Talk to me, Slaney. Tell me what you are thinking." Toryn again waited patiently for Slaney, a quiet thank you to Daci as she set a tray of food in front of them.

Daci watched Slaney as well, recognizing in her some of the traits that the women who came through the shelter displayed. She could and would reach out to her but experience had taught her to be patient and wait for the ladies to speak. She didn't think that it would be any different for Slaney.

"Toryn? Who in your past hates you this much that they would go to all of this trouble? Someone must." Slaney turned her head slightly, discomforted to end up nose to nose with Toryn.

"Who hates me this much? Why would you ask that?" Toryn shared a look with Aidan and Don, hearing the silence in the room as she asked that.

"This has the markings of a hate crime, Toryn. And one of longstanding. I've seen it with the research that I have done and what I have found from Dad's research. This isn't petty and recent. Someone has planned this. I was drawn into your friends' group and then drawn here. An anonymous email suggested that I might want to visit here. I passed it on to the officers in my hometown but they couldn't get anywhere with it. I sent it to Emma, was it just yesterday?" Slaney blinked as she thought through the implications of what she was stating.

"You never mentioned that, Slaney." Aidan's voice was stern. "Send me that email."

Slaney stared at him, trying to stare him down and not succeeding as well as she had hoped. She shrugged and reached for her phone to do that.

"I had forgotten about it, Aidan. I'm sorry. Would it have stopped yesterday if you had had it?" Hope was in her voice that just maybe they were finally getting somewhere.

"It might have, Slaney, but again it might not have. I'll see what the lab techs can do." He frowned at his phone. "On second thought, Emma has already discovered who it is." He looked up at Slaney, his eyes narrowed. "Does James have a brother?"

"James? A brother? Not that I know of. He has a cousin who maintains that he is James' brother but he's not." Horror covered her face. "Is he the one?"

Chapter 36

Aidan turned from the photocopier in his office. He was frustrated, to say the least. He was at a crossroads, he knew, with this case. He was not sure which way to turn. The case was at a standstill, he knew, and had no idea of which way to turn with it. Aidan watched as Lyle walked towards him, a paper in his hand.

"Aidan? What do you make of this?" Lyle handed over the fax that he had been reading.

Aidan took it with a look on his face that said he was ready to pack it all in. That was not a common state for him to be in.

"This fax? It's asking for information on Toryn and Slaney. It's just really bizarre." Lyle waited as Aidan read it over. "What are your thoughts?"

"It's bizarre. It's not how information is normally requested." Aidan rubbed at his cheek. "What do you make of it?"

"Someone is fishing and hoping that we'll oblige them." Lyle saw the moment that Aidan had a plan. "Aidan? What is your plan?"

"That I arrange to meet with this person. I don't do it over the phone or by email or fax. It's in person. I'll talk with both Toryn and Slaney and come up with some answers that might just work." Aidan tapped at the paper. "I'll meet with this person but I'll make sure that I have officers surrounding us. Ben's would work." Aidan grinned as Lyle laughed.

———

"That it would. Go ahead. Keep me in the loop with what you're planning." Lyle was agreeable to Aidan's plan. He knew that it would be thought out well and implemented. That was how Aidan worked.

Aidan made his notes and then reached for his phone. He sent off a quick text to Toryn, just asking where he would find the couple. He was on his feet, searching for George, simply asking him to come with him.

Toryn looked up from where he was sitting on his couch, a frown on his face amid the pain that was showing on it.

"Aidan? You're here? It's over?" Toryn was still not thinking as clearly as he should have been.

"No, it is. Where's Slaney?" Aidan went looking for her, finding her in Toryn's office with Toria. "Slaney? Have you a moment? I need to go over some things with you and Toryn. Toria? You're welcome to join us."

Slaney was on her feet, heading past Aidan and heading for Toryn. Toryn simply wrapped an arm around her as she sat beside him and tucked her close to his side. Toria sat beside Slaney, a questioning look on her face as she glanced first at George and then Aidan.

"Aidan? What do you have?" Toryn broke the uneasy silence in the room.

"First, Toryn, we need to pray. I have some questions to ask you to help implement a plan. God needs to go before us in this." Aidan led the group in prayer with Toryn finishing. They all felt the presence of God in the room when they finished.

"Okay, Aidan. What do you want to talk to us about? Something has come up." Toryn, despite his pain and discomfort, slipped back into his police mode. He knew full well that Aidan would not be there to speak with both himself and Slaney unless something had come up.

"Toryn, we received a fax this morning asking for information about you two."

"A fax? That's not how it's done." Toryn glanced down at Slaney, finding her watching Aidan intently.

"No, it's not. This is what I would like to do." Aidan in turn was watching Slaney, finding her intent gaze somewhat disconcerting. It was not often that happened.

"Why would they do that?" Slaney was working through what that meant.

"They're fishing, Slaney." Aidan looked down at the fax. "Someone has been watching you and Toryn close enough to know that you're friends and are hanging out together. They are trying to find enough information to come at you again. This is what I propose to do." Aidan laid out his plan, sharing a look with Toryn. He was not sure if Toryn would go along with it but it would be Aidan's call to go ahead with it.

Toryn kept his eyes on Aidan, knowing that Aidan was thinking through the plans that he was proposing. It might work. If it did, then just maybe they could find the ones behind it all. He felt Slaney shifting against him and looked down at her, finding her studying her hands.

"I want to be there, Aidan." Slaney was not backing down from him. Toryn had to hide a grin at the dueling looks that the two were giving one another.

"It's not possible, Slaney. That would put you at too much risk." Aidan was prepared to let Toryn and Slaney to be there but put somewhere they could not be seen.

"I will be there, Aidan. If I know where you are meeting, then I will stake out the place 24/7." Slaney was being obstinate. She wanted this over and didn't know how to end it all.

"We'll see, Slaney. Toryn? What are your thoughts?" Aidan waited for Toryn to speak, knowing that Toryn was working through it all.

"Aidan? I think that you have the right idea. Meet with this person in an open area. Talk to him or her to find out what they want. Don't give away any information. If we can be somewhere that we can see the person, one of us might recognize that person. If we can, that may lead to whoever it is that has targeted us. And we are targets, Aidan. Make no mistake about that. We have dribs and drabs on who it is. This may be the one piece that we need. When were you thinking?"

"As soon as I can arrange it. Likely tomorrow or the next day by the latest. I don't want to give too much time. I was thinking at Ben's and having the place full of officers in plain clothes. You two could

———

observe from the kitchen without it being obvious. Ben has done something like this in the past."

"That he has." Toryn nodded, knowing full well that Ben would agree without question. "Is Don on board to be with us?"

"I spoke with him on my way here. He is. They're training but this is the last day for that team." Aidan continued to watch Slaney. "Slaney?"

"Can I see the fax, Aidan, or is that not allowed?" Slaney took the copy of the fax, reading through it. "I know someone who talks like this. From my past." She gave the name, a name that Aidan didn't recognize. "He may be involved to some degree, Aidan. He is friends with James' cousin. You know? The one who is pretending to be his brother?"

"Him? You really think that?" Aidan had been at a loss as to who it could have been. He heard a mutter from George and turned to him. "George?"

"I just got an email from Lyle. He sent one to you as well. They found the cousin. Unfortunately, he's not going to be able to answer any questions. His car was pulled from the lake near Slaney's hometown."

Slaney gave an inaudible exclamation and turned her face into Toryn's shoulder. He could feel the shudders running through her and could only hold her and pray for her. His eyes found George's, who nodded. Toryn sighed. How did they do this now? How did they find the ones behind it all? God was in control, he knew, but sometimes he just wished God would share His plans and purposes for their lives a little bit more.

Chapter 37

Two days later, Toryn walked in the back door to Ben's diner, Slaney's hand tight in his hand. Ben looked around as they entered and pointed towards his office. Don followed them, his team spreading out around the kitchen and the hallway. Aidan had been around early that morning, just confirming what he needed them to do. Slaney had been resistant to his plans but Toryn had promised Aidan that he would keep Slaney out of sight and safe.

Slaney slumped into a chair in Ben's office. She was tired of it all and just wanted it all over. She didn't know if this would end it but she was praying that it would. Slaney had spent the night searching for God's protection and defense for them and for peace and comfort for herself. She had felt that peace this morning but she was quickly losing it as she waited for whatever it was to happen.

Toryn knelt beside her, an arm around her, praying for his lady and then for Aidan and the officers who were out there, putting their lives at risk. His body was still sore and covered in bruises from the explosion. That would take time to heal. It was the emotional burden that he carried that weighed him down and hurt him the most. He didn't like that his lady was hurting so much.

Don tapped at the door and then slid inside, the door closing behind him. He had elected to be the one with them at this point, knowing that his other five team members were mingling in the kitchen and then in the hallway. They would do their best to keep this couple safe.

"Toryn?" Don waited for Toryn to look up at him. "Aidan's here. He's situated himself in the centre of the diner, facing towards the front. Whoever is meeting him has to face the kitchen. Once we have word that the person is here and settled, we'll get you out to take a look at them and then once you've done that, we'll take you to the department building. That is a new request from Aidan. He doesn't want you going home until he has ensured that it is safe for you both to do that.   Toryn, we have your parents somewhere safe. There was word on the street that they would be taken to get to you."

Toryn nodded, knowing that was always a possibility for his parents to disappear. He worried about them all the time it seemed lately. He was grateful for Aidan taking that step for him.

"How long, Don?" Slaney peeked around Toryn to look at Don. "Do we know if that person is here yet?"

"No, we don't. Paul is watching for that. As a cover, he is working as a server. Don't worry. Ben took him in when Paul ended up on the streets. He's worked here for Ben off and on since then. He's the perfect one to have out there. And as well, Ben put out word that the diner was closed for the next few hours and only open for certain customers. Since he's so well liked, he can get away with it." Don grinned at her. "We're taking every precaution to keep everyone safe. The cooks and those in the kitchen know to stay there. We have other officers who have worked here over time working with Paul. That way, we don't have civilians out there. If that's your concern, we have taken that into consideration."

"I thought that you would have. You're too thorough not to have. I just worry about the officers. It's so dangerous for them." Slaney bit at her lip even as Toryn's arm tightened around her.

"We get that, Slaney. We really do. As with all our cases, we attempt with all our strength and might to keep the victim safe. This time, the victims are you and Toryn. It doesn't matter that Toryn is the police chief. He is still a victim. As such, we work with the force to protect him. Sometimes we are not needed. This time, we are. It's what we do, Slaney. While we do training at the moment, our past has been to provide security such as right now to victims. You're not fighting us as some have. And Toryn, I would suspect that you have been speaking with Andrew and Bill both. As officers who went through life and death events of their own, they can help you cope. Just as the ladies are reaching out to you, Slaney, those same ladies are helping you." Don was on his feet and disappearing through the door before Slaney could respond.

Slaney shoved at Toryn, shifting him away from her. She frowned at the look that was in his eyes that said that she was beautiful and his. She thought that she was reading something in them that wasn't true.

"Sit on a chair, Toryn. You're too sore to stay down there on the floor." She was terrified, she had to admit to herself, even though she knew that God was in control. "Where is God in all this, Toryn? I'm having trouble seeing Him in this."

"He's here, Slaney. He always has been. Sometimes we're so close to Him that we don't see Him. We still feel Him with us. He is working in this to bring the culprits to justice. God will use people, such as us, to bring people to justice. I just wish that it hadn't involved you. But if He hadn't, I would not have found you once more. I would have missed that."

Slaney stared at him, her mouth opening and closing. She couldn't believe that he had said that. Her eyes narrowed as he grinned at her for a moment. Despite the closed door, both of the couple could hear the noise from the kitchen and the occasional burst of laughter. Slaney worried about the staff out there, that somehow one of them would be hurt.

Don appeared in the doorway about thirty minutes later, nodding as Toryn rose to his feet.

"We're ready for you, Toryn. Aidan has been meeting with the man for about fifteen minutes. Let's get you out to the kitchen and let you take a peek to see if either of you recognizes him. First, put these on." He handed them both ball caps.

Slaney stared at hers in distaste. She hated caps.

"Put it on, Slaney, or you don't go out. That is one stipulation that Aidan has made. If you don't put it on, you don't go out." Don waited patiently for Slaney to do what he requested.

Slaney finally slapped the cap on her head, finding that Toryn was tugging it down so that the brim shadowed her face. He knew only too well that if they didn't disguise themselves in some way, they may well be recognized. And he didn't want that to happen to Slaney.

Following Don to the kitchen, the couple paused as he held up his hand and made them wait. After a few moments, the couple were moved to stand near the passthrough counter, back far enough that they would seem to be staff but close enough that they could get a look at the man sitting at the table facing Aidan.

Toryn frowned. That man was not known to him. So why would he be asking about him? His eyes dropped to Slaney, watching her closely. He saw the drawn look on her face. She knew the person out there, he decided.

"Slaney? Talk to me. Who is that? And how do you know him?" Toryn's arm around her drew her back into Ben's office. Don and Paul followed, knowing that something had happened and they would more than likely need to reach out to Aidan.

"Him? He's a cousin. I haven't seen him since before my family was killed. I don't know why he's here or why he would want to speak with me. Mom and Dad stopped letting him around us. I just don't know why." She threw herself into Toryn's arms, her own arms tight around his neck.

Toryn caught her close to him, shock on his face. He nodded as Paul walked away, heading for Aidan. Don shut the door behind Paul and then planted himself in front of it. No one would get into the office unless they went through him.

Paul approached the table from behind the man, catching Aidan's eyes. He nodded. Aidan didn't respond but there had been plans put in place if Slaney or Toryn had recognized him. It seemed as if one of them had. Aidan rose, finding officers rising from surrounding tables and approaching him. The man with him looked around before he sighed and stood as well. This had not gone as it was planned, obviously. Now he had to come up with a plausible reason for asking about Slaney and Toryn.

Chapter 38

Toryn paced his house once more that night. He sighed, rubbing at his head. He was sore and hurting physically but more than that, he was hurting for his lady. Slaney had been very quiet as they had been driven home. She had walked away from him, the front door of her home shutting him out. Toryn had not known what to think or say as he watched her.

Don's hand on his shoulder directed Toryn towards his own home. They needed to get him inside and out of sight. His team spread out around the area as did a number of officers. The officers would not be leaving until they were cleared to do so. This was a crisis time for the investigation.

Aidan watched through the window of the interrogation room as the man who had been arrested sat, his head buried in his hands. His head turned as both Lyle and Aaron moved to stand beside him.

"Who's questioning him?" Lyle didn't think that Aidan would, not given his friendship with both Toryn and Slaney.

"George will be. He's just finding some information on him. Toryn got word to me that the man is Slaney's cousin but she hasn't seen him since before her family died."

"Her cousin? Did we know that he was still around?"

Aidan nodded. He had looked into her family and had thought that the cousin was out of the country.

Obviously, at this point, he wasn't. He would be looking further into him.

An hour later, George dropped into the chair in front of Aidan's desk, an inscrutable look on his face. That was unusual for George. Aidan sat back, his pen held in his hand as he watched George.

"George? What did you find out?"

"That he ran away from his parents at fifteen and then left the country when he was twenty. He has had no contact with Slaney since he ran away. He came back when someone from his past contacted him and asked him to reach out to us to find out about Slaney. Toryn seems to be involved in that as well. He wasn't real clear about why he was asked to do that."

"That is strange. Did he give a name?" Aidan waited at George opened a file folder, looked at the paperwork inside it, closed the folder, and then handed it over.

"This is what he said. It's not making a lot of sense. I wish that it was over for them but it doesn't seem to be." George waited as Aidan read the information.

"This man?" Aidan looked up, shock on his face. "He's involved?"

"He is. And he knows Toryn well." George looked up at the ceiling. He knew that they needed to talk with Toryn. He just didn't want to be the one to do that.

"What information do we have on him?"

"Not a lot. I've asked Emma to look into him for us. She's put in as a priority. Once we have that information or by tomorrow morning at the latest, you and I are heading his way. Slaney needs to be part of that conversation." George sighed. This was not how life was to be. He was getting tired of friends being involved in situations such as this.

Aidan nodded. He would be working through the night just as George would be.

"George? Head out and grab us a meal." Aidan handed over some bills. "We need to work on this and we're going to be here for quite a while, I suspect."

Early the next morning, Aidan rose and walked over to his printer, grabbing the papers that it was spewing out. He tapped them into a pile and then walked away from his office, heading for Aaron. Aaron had not left either, paperwork keeping him there as he waited for Aidan and George to finish what they needed to do.

"Aaron? This is what we have." Aidan handed it over, knowing that Toryn would not be happy with what they had found. This involved some officers and lab techs. He had suspected that himself but had not suspected the ones involved.

Aaron studied Aidan closely, seeing the upset on Aidan's face. He took the paperwork and began to read through it. His face tightened as he read the names.

"You're sure on this?" Aaron looked up as he asked his question. He could hear voices and movement outside of his office door. This was really going to hurt the people that he worked with.

"We are. We've gone back over and over it. Emma sent confirmation of this for us. We need to arrest fellow officers and that is not going to be pleasant. Toryn will feel it. To think that officers and techs are involved with this man." Aidan was disturbed greatly by that.

"They're new to the force, aren't they? Toryn is not as close to those ones as he is to the ones who have been officers and employees for a number of years. Let me know when you're heading for him and I'll go with you. Make sure that Slaney is there. She needs to know how this is all connecting."

"She will be. Toryn will make sure of that. He's in love with her and she with him, but neither will say anything until this is all over." Aidan had been watching his friends closely.

"Yes, they are. Tavin and Toria are safe?"

"They are. Abe and some of his team came and took them to his place. It's secure there." Aidan had been glad for Abe's offer to do that. It relieved his mind to know that they were safe.

Two hours later, Aidan reached for his jacket. It was a day that was drizzling rain and it seemed to suit his mood. He picked up his folders and then headed for Aaron.

"Aaron?" Aidan's voice brought the man's head up before Aaron was on his feet and reaching for his own jacket.

"You're ready to go." Aaron's words were a statement and not a question.

"I am. I don't like this, Aaron. We're moving forward but we still don't have the name of the man or woman who is in charge. And when we start with the arrests, that will set him off even more." Aidan paused as he pulled to a stop in Toryn's driveway. "I asked that Slaney be taken to Toryn's home. I gather that she was not too happy about being woken up."

Aaron grinned for a moment. They were beginning to see the lady who was Slaney. She had been hidden for far too long, he decided. And what he was seeing made him sure that she was just who Toryn needed in his life. She was not backing down from the chief and that was who he needed.

Toryn stood just inside his open front door, watching as Aidan and Aaron walked towards him. He too had been woken up by an officer who had simply stated that the two men were on their way there. He had hugged Slaney as she had entered his home before she shoved away from him and headed for the kitchen. Slaney was intent on preparing breakfast of some kind for them all. She just knew that they needed it. Her heart was rising in desperate prayer.

Chapter 39

Toryn reached for Slaney's hand an hour later, refusing to let it go as she tugged at it. Instead, he pulled her with him despite her protests to his office where he shoved her to a seat on the couch. She glared at him as he sat beside her. Neither saw the amused looks that quickly flittered across the others' faces.

Aidan looked around the office, his eyes taking in the packed bookshelves, the framed photos on the walls, the certificates, and then the comfortable furnishings. The soft green walls suited Toryn, he decided. He always found himself relaxing in this room.

"Aidan? What did you find?" Toryn was on the offensive. He wanted this over and over that very day if possible. "It can't be good. I know you too well to know that it's other than that."

"It's not good, Toryn. George interviewed Ted Brookes, Slaney's cousin. He had been living in another country all these years until the last month. He was paid to come back here and try to find Slaney. If he found Slaney, he was to draw her away from safety and she would be taken away from here. This was partly because of the columns that her father wrote and secondly? It was to get to you, Toryn."

"I don't understand, Aidan." Slaney frowned at the detective. "Why would that be?"

"Because they connected you two from your university days. Apparently, you two would sit beside each other quite often. They thought that you were dating." Aidan watched with compassion as Slaney frowned at him. "We know that you weren't and that you were just acquaintances. Your cousin ran away when he was young because he wanted to leave your town and his parents wouldn't let him."

"No, they wouldn't let him. I often wondered what happened to him. I didn't trust him a lot, just because there was something about him." Slaney leaned against Toryn without realizing that she was seeking comfort from him.

"And you were wise not to. From what Emma has found out, he lived a life of crime in his new country. He is still in custody, Toryn, awaiting for word from overseas if he needs to be returned there. Also, if we keep him in custody, he can't get to either one of you. And that was what he was ordered to do." Aidan looked down at the folders that he had on his knee. "Toryn, we have discovered that there are some officers and civilian employees involved in this. It's not what we wanted to find."

Toryn had already come to that conclusion. He reached for the folders, a prayer rising within him. He knew that once he read what Aidan had provided, there was no going back to what it had been. He frowned down at Slaney who was watching Aidan and Aaron closely.

Reading through the paperwork, Toryn paused at the last page. He noted the names. They were all recent recruits and not in any position of true authority. The civilian employees were also recent hires and not in a place where they could do any harm.

"Aaron?" Toryn looked at the deputy chief, knowing well how he would feel.

"I know, Toryn. There are only about six or so that we have found. There may be more but for now, I have asked that our detectives bring them in and question them. That is being done even as we're meeting. I'm sorry."

"I know you are. We had no idea, did we? Are they involved in that robbery?" Toryn was running scenarios in his mind, trying to determine just how much damage had been done.

"Not that we can see. But they seem to have been placed here for a reason. And that reason is you and indirectly Slaney."

"Toryn, if you were not the chief, what would happen? Would Aaron take over?" Slaney had been reading the paperwork as well.

"No, he wouldn't. He would act as the chief just as he is now. But they would advertise and then hire a chief. That could be what they were wanting to do."

"If they discredit you, then they could bring in someone that could corrupt the force?" Slaney was thinking through the implications of what Toryn had been facing.

"That is true, Slaney." Aaron shared a look with Toryn. They could all hear the early morning sounds of nature coming through the open windows and felt the slight warm breeze that stirred through the room.

"I see. But I don't know why I became involved. Do you?" Slaney was desperate to know that she was not the reason for all of this.

"We're getting a picture of that, Slaney. For some reason, whoever it is decided that you and Toryn were close during your university days. Your cousin explained that to us. Now as to what has happened now? The robbers saw you and then saw Toryn. They were well aware of who you both were. They started to chase you, knowing that Toryn would come to your rescue. He did exactly what they had wanted. You were not to be shot, Toryn. You moved into their line of fire and were hit." Aaron looked up at Toryn, seeing the shuttered look on his face. "That we have confirmed. Now, as to who it is, do you have any thoughts?"

Toryn sighed. He had been praying it through over the night before and had come up with a name. He reached for the slip of paper sitting on the table beside him. He handed it to Aidan, waiting for Aidan to read it and react.

Aidan took the paper that Toryn was handing him. His eyes dropped to it and he drew in a deep breath. It was not who he had expected.

"You're sure about this?" Aidan drew in a deep breath as Toryn nodded. "Then, we have some work to do. He's kept himself quite hidden."

"Not really." Toryn knew that because he grew up in the town where he now served as the police chief, he was more aware of the undercurrents that ran through it. He looked down at Slaney, finding her watching him in return. His arm tightened around her, knowing that this was crunch time as it was called. "Emma had pegged him as well. She said that she was sending over a lot of information on him that she's been able to find."

"And she will." Aidan sat back, lost in thought. "How do we draw him out?"

"I do that, Aidan. It has to be that way. We don't have any choice other than that. Slaney and I will do that. We just need to come up with a plan on how to do that." Toryn's head dropped for a moment as he prayed for his lady. This was a dangerous stunt for them to try and without doing that, they would have to live in hiding for months.

Chapter 40

A week later, Toryn walked through the downtown area. He was back at work and out doing what he always did, checking in with the businesses in the downtown section. Toryn had started this practice when he became chief and had missed his interaction with the business owners and employees.

Slaney waited for him to approach her, a hug and then a kiss on her cheek from Toryn. She had begun to expect that from him. Toryn had clearly told her two days prior that he was going to be dating her, whether she agreed to that or not. She had stared at him, her mouth open until he gently tapped her under her chin.

"Toryn! It's too dangerous!" Slaney protested even though his words warmed her heart and gave her hope for the future.

"It doesn't matter, sweetheart. You're the lady who I love and want in my life. God knows how long our days are. Murphy from Abe's team tells us that God has a plan and purpose for our lives that we don't know as yet. I would like to think that God planned for us to meet again and that it is in His plan that we spend the rest of our lives together. We take one day at a time. Will you be my lady?" Toryn waited patiently for Slaney to puzzle and think his request through, her hands tight in his.

Slaney had finally nodded, knowing that Toryn had put himself out there in front of her. She struggled to release her hands before she hugged him.

Toryn looked up at last, a grin on his face as he approached Slaney. This had not been planned but here was his lady. He had gone to the police services board and simply told them that he was dating Slaney and that he loved her. If necessary, he was prepared to leave his position. None of them had agreed with that, having observed Toryn and Slaney over the past few weeks. They knew full well that Toryn and Slaney were a couple. Toryn was also well loved and respected by the force. They would not want him to walk away from them but he would if he felt it necessary.

"Hello, sweetheart." Toryn dropped a kiss on her cheek. "Meeting someone for lunch?"

"I am. There's this tall and handsome police chief in Oak City who seems to think that he needs my time and attention. I was going to meet him for lunch but since you're here, you'll do." Slaney grinned as Toryn shook a finger at her.

"Well, then, sweetheart. Let's see what Ben has to offer today." He opened the door for her and followed her in, a hand raised to wave at Ben.

Slaney slid over on the bench seat in a booth, knowing that Toryn would sit beside her. It was how it was when they went out now. She was thanking God daily for the man who had appeared in her life once more. She had admired and respected him when they were in university. She had not expected him to come back into her life, save that very life, and then become such a huge part of her daily walk.

Ben approached Toryn as the couple finished their meal, sliding onto the seat across from them. He studied them, knowing that as happy as they seemed right now, he had news that would change that. He stared down at the envelope he had placed on the tabletop before sliding it across the table to Toryn.

Toryn reached to pick up the envelope, tucking it into a pocket before he was on his feet, his hand reaching for Slaney's. He tugged her with him towards the police department building, finding a visitor's badge for her before heading for his office. Toryn waved for Aidan to follow him.

The door shut behind the three, Toryn retrieved the envelope. Ben had not said anything but he didn't need to. This is something that Ben has done in the past. He opened it, read it, and then passed it on to Aidan. Toryn then moved to crouch beside Slaney's chair.

"Toryn? What is that all about?" Slaney studied him, trusting him completely, but also anxious to know what had just happened.

"That was a letter from someone on the streets. He has reached out to us before. He has confirmed our suspicions. We will be moving in to arrest the man who is behind all this. We just need to keep ourselves tucked away and safe." His hand reached to rest on her cheek, feeling her leaning against his hand.

"Okay. How long?"

"As long as it takes. If it goes too late tonight, then we find somewhere safe to stay and come back and do this all over again tomorrow." Toryn was on his feet, heading for Aaron, Aidan keeping pace with him. A female officer had moved to stand at the doorway to keep watch over Toryn's beloved Slaney.

"Aaron? Streeter came through." Toryn handed over the letter. "Aidan has enough now he tells me, to go for the warrants that he needs."

"Good. We need this over with. But you do know that he's not going to be where you think he will be." Aaron gave a grim smile. They had been through this too many times to think that would how it would play out.

"We know that. Streeter and his friends are following him, he tells me. And that will be what we need." Toryn was away, working with his teams to set up what they needed to and choosing who would go where. He stepped back at last, exhausted but confident that in the next day or so, the man would be in custody and he could begin to live his life again. And that life would include his lady, Slaney.

Slaney slumped against Toryn's shoulder that evening. They had not found the man as yet despite their searches. She and Toryn were headed for a safe house, Don's team moving in to assist the officers assigned to protect them. She had a great sense of fear, though. She was afraid for the men and women who were with them. She was also greatly afraid for Toryn. This was it, Slaney understood. This was when it all came together and they found out the reason why. She wanted to know if this person had been responsible for the deaths of her family. Somehow, she seemed to believe that he was. Slaney just didn't know if she was ready to hear that and to hear the reason why. It had been so many years and it had taken so much from her.

Chapter 41

Toryn walked slowly towards the house where they were to spend the night. Slaney's hand was tight in his. He could sense the fatigue in her as her steps were slow. He wanted this over for his lady but he didn't know if that would be on the morrow or for more days than they wanted to give to this man.

His steps slowed as he stepped through the door and into the hallway. Something was off, he felt. He just didn't know what. Toryn sensed Slaney's hesitation to enter any further. He frowned and spun as the door shut behind him. He felt the danger that was awaiting them in the house. Spinning, Toryn struggled to open the door again but was unable to. It just would not budge. He could feel Slaney's hand on his back before he spun back towards her. He shoved her forward towards the back door. Only this door didn't open either. He could hear pounding from the outside and yells for him to open the door.

Heavy footsteps sounded behind them. Toryn spun once more to face the man, shoving Slaney behind him. Her hand gripped his shirt tightly and he said afterwards that he thought that she had actually grasped his flesh.

"Who are you?" Toryn's voice sounded loud in the quiet of the house.

"You know who I am, Knight. This ends now and right here. So nice that Slaney is with you. I'll take care of two problems at the same time." Dale Boyce moved closer to the chief, a weapon raised and pointed at Toryn's head. "Too bad it had to come to this point."

"I don't understand. What did I ever do to you?" Toryn stood his ground, watching Boyce but also watching for a way to get Slaney out of there. It would just take a few seconds for that to happen. It didn't matter if he was hurt just so that Slaney was safe. He could still hear the pounding at the doors.

"What did you ever do to me? I'll tell you." Boyce was at the point that spittle was flying from his mouth. His hand holding his weapon was wavering. This was a dangerous point for the couple. Boyce was out of control and Toryn knew just how much of a predicament that he and Slaney were in.

"Tell me, Boyce. Tell me." Toryn was taunting the man, knowing that it was not a great move but he felt he had no choice. He could also feel the presence of God in the room and afterwards was sure that he saw angels surrounding them. Slaney shared that impression as well.

Boyce stared at Toryn and then shifted slightly to the side to where he could see Slaney. He had them where he wanted them and he would take full advantage of that.

"Why am I after you? You weren't supposed to live when you were a teenager. You turned in the son of a friend of mine for drug dealing. I've been plotting since then to bring you down. You were supposed to be with your friends that night they had that accident. You were to die in that. Instead, you refused to go with them because of your "church" duties. I followed you to university and plotted to bring you down there. Only, I couldn't do that. I couldn't get close enough to you. I saw you and Slaney together and decided that she would be used to bring you down. Only, she never showed up here until now. She was too well hidden. Her father wrote a column about a murder that I had done years ago. That's why they died."

Slaney could not control the sob that escaped her before her head was burrowed against Toryn. This was why her parents and brother had died. This man had done that in revenge.

"But you didn't find Slaney that night." Toryn drew in a deep breath. He thought he heard snapping wood at the front of the house and prayed that it was help coming in and not Boyce's henchman.

"No, the men couldn't and they didn't understand why." Boyce frowned. It had been a mystery that had haunted him for all those years.

"She hid, Boyce, under her bed. God kept her safe." Toryn moved slightly to the side, Slaney shuffling with him. "But tell me. The robbers who shot the officers? They were your men?"

"They were. That was planned to draw you out to the scene. But you showed up and were surrounded by officers. I couldn't get to you." Boyce was growing more unstable the more that they talked. "The men who were killed? They meant nothing to me. You do. I want your blood for what you did." His weapon pointed towards Toryn's chest, aiming for his heart. "And Slaney needs to pay for her father's work."

Toryn gave a shout and threw himself sideways, his arms wrapping around Slaney. He heard the discharge of the weapon and then shouts that were unintelligible. He felt hands on him, raising him to his feet and then shoving him out of the back door. Toryn refused to let go of Slaney, an arm wrapped around her. They were shoved into the back seat of a patrol car which took off as soon as the doors slammed shut. They were heading back for Toryn's office.

Aidan came to find Toryn two hours later. Slaney was sound asleep in Toryn's arms, his head resting on hers. His eyes found Aidan as Aidan sat down near them, exhaustion in his being.

"Aidan?" Toryn spoke at last, his voice quiet but just loud enough to waken Slaney. She stirred in his arms, rubbing at her face and then focusing on Aidan.

"It's over, Toryn. He put up a fight and shot at us. We had no choice but to return fire."

"Were any officers hurt?" Toryn drew in a deep breath of relief when Aidan shook his head. "We won't know exactly what all he planned, will we?"

"We will. We served the search warrants on his wife. She's glad he's not around any more. I referred her to see Daci." Aidan didn't say anything more but he didn't need to. Both men understood that Boyce's wife had been a battered woman.

"I don't understand how he found out about Dad's column." Slaney spoke, her voice hesitant to even ask a question.

"Someone in James' office took money to tell him that. That man was killed as well once he could not serve Boyce any longer. Boyce never knew that you were writing the columns, Slaney. That is something that will go no further than this office. If anyone has any suspicions, then they will remain just as that. I spoke with James. He was horrified to hear that he had been inadvertently involved in your family's death. I think that he had suspicions and part of that was why he insisted that you keep as low a profile as you could. That's not going to work now though." He gave a grin at her as she frowned. "You're dating the police chief, Slaney. That puts you out there."

Slaney shifted to look up at Toryn, finding him watching her. He dropped a kiss on her forehead and she just snuggled closer to him.

"That I don't mind, Aidan. In fact, I am looking forward to being able to move around freely and not have to look over my shoulder. Thank you, Aidan, you and everyone else who worked on this. You have solved a mystery from my past as well as solving the mystery surrounding these events." She yawned, turned her face more into Toryn's shoulder, and slept.

Toryn had a tender smile on his face as he watched his sweetheart sleep.

"My thanks, Aidan." He looked up at his friend. "You went above and beyond. I don't understand, though, how he knew where we would be."

"Another mole in the department. We arrested one of the clerks in the booking office. She heard the place where we were planning on taking you and let him know. I pray that we have found everyone now."

Aidan was on his feet, moving away, fatigue weighing him down. He yawned and then reached for his car keys. He was heading home for a few hours of sleep and would be back in the morning. All seemed right once more in Oak City.

Three months later, Slaney turned from her front door and walked after Toryn as he headed for the kitchen. He had brought a meal that Ben had insisted that they needed. She drew in a deep breath, the aroma of the meal making her hungry.

Toryn set the bag with the meal down and turned, simply sweeping Slaney into his arms and kissing her. He didn't let her go right away, finding her hugging him back. He was content. The adventure that they had been involved in was over. He had found the lady with whom he wanted to spend the rest of his life.

"Toryn? How was today?" Slaney set out their meal and then sat beside Toryn, taking the hand that he was reaching out to her.

"It was good." He bowed his head to ask the blessing on their food. "The officers are back almost to where they were before all this. We'll never be the same. Losing friends and colleagues does that to you."

"It does. Dad used to say that when he would write some of his columns. I get that sense as well with mine." She bit into her salad, chewed the mouthful, and then swallowed. "You're different tonight."

"Am I?" Toryn grinned at the pretend frown she sent his way. "Would you like to go for a walk after we finish?"

"I would like that, Toryn. But before we do, we need to spend time in prayer. God protected us and I can't say thanks to Him enough."

"No, we can't say thanks enough."

An hour later, Slaney nestled her hand tighter into Toryn's grip. She sensed that he was wanting to talk and she was afraid that he would say that he didn't want to date her any more.

Toryn pointed to a bench in a nearby parkette. It was a favourite spot for them to sit and be silent with one another. He bit at his lip. He had been by his parents' home the night before. His mother had cornered him and handed him a small jeweller's box. He knew what was in it. It was the ruby ring that had been her mother's. Toria had been given it to hold onto for Toryn's bride. That had been the stipulation her mother had given her.

"Toryn? You're quiet tonight." Slaney had to break the silence. It seemed to have gone on for too long.

"I am. Slaney, when I saw you that day, I think I recognized you before I realized that it was you. I tried to get you away. Only that didn't work out so well." He stared down at the gravel path near his feet. "I felt a connection with you even when we were just acquaintances at university. I think I had been looking for you ever since. I never dated, never wanted to." He looked up to find her gaze intent on him. "Slaney, I do love you. You are the one God had in mind for me. Will you marry me, be my best friend and helpmeet for however long God grants us?"

Tears blinded Slaney for a moment. All she could do was nod. Her vision cleared as she felt Toryn's fingers on hers and then watched as he slid a beautiful ruby ring on her finger.

"This was my grandmother's. She gave it to Mom for my bride. Will you wear it?"

"I will, Toryn. I am honoured to do so. And yes, I will marry you if you will be my best friend and guardian and protector for as long as we live."

Toryn kissed his sweetheart and then settled back with her in his arms. They didn't talk, these two. There would be time for talking. For now, they were content in the new love that was surrounding them and welling up within them. God had brought them together and would walk with them through all their days. They had no doubt about that.

Slaney stirred at last, her eyes on the trees surrounding them. The sun was beginning to set but she was content.

"Toryn, you have wonderful friends and colleagues. The ladies are taking me into their group. Phoebe calls me at least twice a week." She looked up at him. "We need to go and see them."

"And we will. Tomorrow night, Mom and Dad want us to come for a meal, if that's okay."

"It's more than okay. Your parents are just so wonderful. I miss mine and always will and I miss my brother. Your parents have stepped in to help fill that gap."

"I'm glad, sweetheart. Mom always wanted a daughter but they were content with just the family that God gave them. They never let me feel anything less than loved and wanted." Toryn was on his feet, his hand reaching to help Slaney to her feet. "We need to plan a wedding, sweetheart. Don't let it be too long." He frowned as Slaney began to laugh. "Did I say something funny?"

Slaney giggled once more before she shook her head.

"Between your mom and the ladies, our wedding is planned. Your mom's dress fits me. So we can get married tomorrow if you want." She hugged him before her hand was back in his.

"We could, could we? I think we need to let you enjoy being engaged at least for a day or so." He avoided the elbow that she threw at him. "We'll talk it over, sweetheart. For now, we need to get you home."

Toryn turned his phone over and over that night, knowing that he needed to make a phone call but not sure how to express himself.

"Phoebe?" His voice was hesitant.

Phoebe stared at Andrew before she grinned as he smiled back at her.

"Toryn? You asked?"

"I did, Phoebe, and she said yes. I know that Mom and the ladies are helping but would you reach out to Slaney?"

"I'd be glad to do that. Tomorrow is Saturday, Toryn. How be we come and find you two?"

Toryn sat back, his eyes on the photo of Slaney that sat on his desk. He was in love and his lady loved him back. He reached for his phone and smiled at the goodnight that Slaney had texted to him. He responded, knowing that in just a few weeks they would be together. His head bowed as he thanked God for His protection over the past weeks and months and that He had blessed both he and Slaney with the loves of their lives.

Thank you for choosing to read the story of Toryn and his lady, Slaney. Toryn appeared in Andrew and Phoebe's story first as her beloved cousin who was not a cousin after all. He became vocal in the stories of Don and his team, simply stating that he had a story to tell. And he did.

When I wrote the first few chapters of this story, it was back in December, 2022. Since that time, here in Canada, unfortunately we have had police officers who have died in the line of duty. This is a sad time for all who had lost family members and friends as well as colleagues.

This story has evolved on its own. Once more, the characters have simply told their story as they wanted to. I never plan out a story because I know that it will change. What I think may work in one story usually doesn't until one later one.

Toryn and his Slaney faced difficulties and danger just because of the hatred of one man. God was there with them through it all. It doesn't matter what we face. We are never alone. God is there with us each step of the way. He never leaves us or forsakes us.

Now, as to the characters who walked into the story, just like always. Abe and Emma and his team's stories are *His Guardians*. Andrew and Phoebe's story is *The Potter's Hands*. Bill and Cora's is *Hidden in the*

Hollow. Don's team is *His Defenders*. Richard's team is *His Protectors*. I never plan for them to appear but they always do. My characters just seem to be friends with one another. The men from The Barnabas Foundation are found in *The Barnabas Chronicles*.

God bless each one of you. May His presence be felt with you each and any day.

Ronna